GODSGRAVE

THE NEVERNIGHT CHRONICLE

BOOK II

JAY KRISTOFF

 ST. MARTIN'S GRIFFIN NEW YORK

GODSGRAVE. Copyright © 2017 by Neverafter PTY LTD. All rights reserved. Printed in the United States of America. For information, address St. Martin's Press, 175 Fifth Avenue, New York, N.Y. 10010.

www.stmartins.com

Designed by Steven Seighman

Typography by Meg Morley

Trinity logo by James Orr

Maps by Virginia Allyn

The Library of Congress has cataloged the hardcover edition as follows:

Names: Kristoff, Jay, author.
Title: Godsgrave / Jay Kristoff.
Description: First edition. | New York : St. Martin's Press, 2017. | Series: Nevernight chronicle ; Book 2
Identifiers: LCCN 2017021359 | ISBN 9781250073037 (hardcover) | ISBN 9781466885042 (ebook)
Subjects: LCSH: Imaginary wars and battles—Fiction. | Assassins—Fiction. | Revenge—Fiction. | GSAFD: Fantasy fiction.
Classification: LCC PR9619.4.K74 G63 2017 | DDC 823/.92—dc23
LC record available at https://lccn.loc.gov/2017021359

ISBN 978-1-250-17014-9 (trade paperback)

Our books may be purchased in bulk for promotional, educational, or business use. Please contact your local bookseller or the Macmillan Corporate and Premium Sales Department at 1-800-221-7945, extension 5442, or by email at MacmillanSpecialMarkets@macmillan.com.

First St. Martin's Griffin Edition: June 2018

11

For my enemies
I couldn't have done it without you

THE REPUBLIC OF
ITREYA

N

SEA OF SILENCE

STORMWA

DAWN

WHITE

CITY OF
GODSGRAVE

SEA

TAL

FARROW

SEAWALL

ISLES OF DWEYM

NALIPSE

TSANA

THE SWORD ARM

THE SPINE

THE HEART

THE SEA OF SILENCE

GODSGRAVE
CATHEDRAL

MERCURIO'S
CURIOS

LIISIAN MARKET

THE BAY OF
BUTCHERS

WESTERN NETHERS

THE BRIDGE OF FOLLIES

THE SHIELD ARM

THE AQUEDUCT

HE RIBS

THE WHITE PALAZZO

THE PHILOSOPHER'S STONE

N

EASTERN NETHERS

GODSGRAVE

THE CITY OF BRIDGES AND BONES

G OF ITREYA

CROW'S REST

SEA OF SWORDS

CROW'S NEST

Good turn to you, gentlefriends. It's lovely to see you again.

I confess, I missed you in our time apart. And now, reunited, would that I could simply greet you with a smile, and let you be about the business of murder and revenge and occasional lashings of tastefully written smut. But before we slip back between the pages together, I should impart a warning true.

Memory is a traitor, and a liar, and a good-for-nothing thief. And though our drama's cast is doubtless inked indelibly on your psyche, we must sometimes make allowances for the lesser among you mortals.

So, perhaps a refresher is in order?

Dramatis Personae

Mia Corvere—assassin, thief, and heroine of our tale—if our tale can be said to have one at all. Her father, Darius, was executed under order of the Itreyan Senate and, vowing vengeance, she became a disciple of the Republic's most feared cult of assassins, the Red Church.

Though she failed the Church's trials, Mia was inducted as a Blade (aka assassin) after rescuing the Church's ministry during an assault by Luminatii legionaries.

Mia is of mixed Itreyan-Liisian blood. She is also darkin—one who controls the darkness itself. She has little understanding of her powers, and the only other darkin she has ever met died before he could give her the answers she desired.

Tragic, I know.

Mister Kindly—a daemon, passenger, or familiar (depending on who one asks) made of shadows, who eats Mia's fear. He saved her life as a child, and claims to know very little about his true nature, though he's been known to lie from time to time.

He wears the shape of a cat, though he is nothing close to a cat at all.

Eclipse—another shadow daemon, who wears the guise of a wolf. Eclipse was passenger to Lord Cassius, former head of the Red Church. When Cassius died during the Luminatii assault, Eclipse bound herself to Mia instead.

Like most dogs and cats, she and Mister Kindly do not get along.

Old Mercurio—Mia's trainer and confidant in the time before she joined the Red Church. Mercurio was a Church Blade himself for many years, but is now retired in Godsgrave. The old Itreyan runs a store named Mercurio's Curios and serves as an information broker and talent scout for the servants of the Black Mother.

A grumpier old bastard was never found under any of the three suns.

Tric—an acolyte of the Red Church, also Mia's friend and lover. Tric was of mixed Itreyan-Dweymeri heritage. He was poised to be inducted into the Blades, but Ashlinn Järnheim stabbed him repeatedly in the heart and pushed him off the side of the Quiet Mountain.

As a promise to Tric, Mia assassinated Tric's grandfather, Swordbreaker, king of the Dweymeri Isles, after the boy's death.

Which wasn't all that sensible, when you think about it . . .

Ashlinn Järnheim—an acolyte of the Red Church and formerly one of Mia's closest friends. Ash was born in Vaan, and is the daughter of Torvar Järnheim, a retired Blade of the Church. As vengeance for a maiming he received in the Mother's service, he and his children hatched a plot that almost brought the entire Church to its knees, though their conspiracy was finally foiled by Mia.

Ash's brother, Osrik, was killed in the process, but Ashlinn escaped.

Ash's feelings about Mia are best described as . . . complicated.

Naev—a Hand (aka disciple) of the Red Church and close friend of Mia, who manages supply runs in the desolate Whisperwastes of Ysiir. Naev was disfigured by Weaver Marielle out of jealousy, but as reward for Mia's assistance during the Luminatii assault, Marielle restored Naev's former beauty.

Naev never forgets and never forgives—one of the reasons she and Mia get along.

Drusilla—Revered Mother of the Red Church and, despite her apparent old age, one of the deadliest servants of the Black Mother alive. Drusilla failed Mia in her final trial, and it was only after the intercession of Cassius, Lord of Blades, that the girl was inducted.

To put it kindly, she is not Mia's greatest fan.

Solis—Shahiid of Songs, trainer of Red Church acolytes in the art of steel.

Mia cut his face during their first sparring session. Solis hacked off her arm in retaliation.

They get along swimmingly now, as you can imagine.*

Spiderkiller—voted "Shahiid Most Likely to Murder Her Own Students" five years running, Spiderkiller is mistress of the Hall of Truth. Mia was one of her most promising acolytes, but after she failed Drusilla's final test, Spiderkiller's fondness for the girl has all but evaporated.

Mouser—Shahiid of Pockets and master of thievery. Charming, witty, and as fond of larceny as he is of wearing ladies' underthings. The Itreyan has no strong enmity toward Mia, which practically makes him the leader of her fan club.

Aalea—Shahiid of Masks and mistress of secrets. It is said there are only two types of folk in this world: those who love Aalea, and those who've yet to meet her.

She actually seems quite fond of Mia.

Shocking, aye?

Marielle—one of two albino sorcerii in the service of the Church. Marielle is a master of the ancient Ysiiri magik of flesh weaving, capable of sculpting skin and muscle as if it were clay. However, the toll she pays for her power is a steep one—her own flesh is hideous to behold, and she has no power to change it.

Marielle cares for no one save her brother Marius, and he, perhaps too much.

Marius—the second sorcerii who serves the Quiet Mountain. Marius is a blood speaker, capable of manipulating human vitus. Thanks to his sister's arts, he is handsome beyond compare.

Though, I do recall a saying about books and covers . . .

Aelius—the chronicler of the Quiet Mountain, charged with maintaining some semblance of order in the Red Church's great Athenaeum.

Like everything else in Niah's library, Aelius is dead.

He seems a little ambivalent about the fact.

---

*Yes, gentlefriends, that was sarcasm. Admit it, you missed me, didn't you?

Hush—a former acolyte of the Red Church, now a full-fledged Blade. Hush never speaks, instead communicating through a form of sign language known as Tongueless.

The Itreyan boy assisted Mia in her final trials, though he'd insist they are not friends.

Jessamine Gratianus—a Red Church acolyte from Mia's crop who failed to become a Blade. Jessamine is the daughter of Marcinus, an Itreyan centurion executed for his loyalty to Mia's father, Darius "the Kingmaker" Corvere. Jess blames Darius, and by extension, Mia herself, for her father's death—though in truth, the girls have much in common.

The desire to see Consul Julius Scaeva gutted like a pig, for example.

Julius Scaeva—thrice-elected consul of the Itreyan Senate. Scaeva has maintained sole consulship since the Kingmaker Rebellion six years ago. The position is usually shared, and consuls sit only one term, but with Scaeva, the rules seem not to apply.

He presided over the execution of Mia's father, and sentenced her mother and baby brother to die in the Philosopher's Stone. He also ordered Mia drowned in a canal.

Yes, he's something of a cunt.

Francesco Duomo—grand cardinal of the Church of the Light, and the most powerful member of the Everseeing's ministry. Along with Scaeva and Remus, he was responsible for passing sentence on the Kingmaker rebels.

Duomo is the right hand of Aa upon this earth. The mere sight of a holy relic blessed by a man of his conviction is enough to send Mia writhing in agony.

Stabbing the bleeding fuck out of him may prove problematic as a result.

Justicus Marcus Remus—former justicus of the Luminatii Legion, and leader of the attack on the Quiet Mountain. During his climactic confrontation with Mia, Remus made several cryptic remarks about Mia's brother, Jonnen.

Mia stabbed the Itreyan to death before he could fully explain himself.

He was not pleased.

Alinne Corvere—Mia's mother. Though she was born in Liis, Alinne rose to prominence in the halls of Itreyan power. She was a political genius, and a dona of no little esteem and will. Imprisoned in the Philosopher's Stone with her infant son after her husband's failed rebellion, she died in madness and misery.

Yes, I quite liked her, too.

Darius "the Kingmaker" Corvere—Mia's father. Former justicus of the Luminatii Legion, Darius forged an alliance with General Gaius Maxinius Antonius that would have seen Antonius crowned as king. Together, the two Itreyans raised an army and marched on their own capital, but were both captured on the eve of battle. Without leadership, their army shattered. Their troops were crucified, and Darius himself was hung with his would-be king Antonius beside him.

So close they could almost touch.

Jonnen Corvere—Mia's brother. An infant at the time of his father's rebellion, Jonnen was imprisoned with his mother in the Stone at the order of Julius Scaeva. He died there before Mia ever had a chance to rescue him.

Aa—the Father of Light, also known as the Everseeing. The three suns, known as Saan (the Seer), Saai (the Knower), and Shiih (the Watcher), are said to be his eyes, and one or more is usually present in the heavens, with the result that actual nighttime, or truedark, occurs for only one week every two and a half years.

Aa is a beneficent god, kind to his subjects and merciful to his enemies. And if you believe that one, gentlefriends, I've a bridge in Godsgrave to sell you.

Tsana—Lady of Fire, She Who Burns Our Sin, the Pure, Patron of Women and Warriors, and firstborn daughter of Aa and Niah.

Keph—Lady of Earth, She Who Ever Slumbers, the Hearth, Patron of Dreamers and Fools, and secondborn of Aa and Niah.

Trelene—Lady of Oceans, She Who Will Drink the World, the Fate, Patron of Sailors and Scoundrels, thirdborn daughter of Aa and Niah, and twin to Nalipse.

Nalipse—Lady of Storms, She Who Remembers, the Merciful, Patron of Healers and Leaders, fourthborn of Aa and Niah, and twin to Trelene.

Niah—the Mother of Night, Our Lady of Blessed Murder, also known as the Maw. Sisterwife of Aa, Niah rules a lightless region of the hereafter known as the Abyss. She and Aa initially shared the rule of the sky equally. Commanded to bear her husband only daughters, Niah eventually disobeyed Aa's edict and bore him a son. In punishment, she was banished from the skies by her beloved, allowed to return only for a brief spell every few years.

And as for what became of their son?

As I said last time, gentlefriends, that would be spoiling things.

The wolf does not pity the lamb,
And the storm begs no forgiveness of the
drowned.
—RED CHURCH MANTRA

BOOK 1

THE RED PROMISE

PERFUME

Nothing stinks quite like a corpse.

It takes a while for them to really start reeking. O, chances are good if you don't soil your britches before you die, you'll soil them soon afterward—your human bodies simply work that way, I'm afraid. But I don't mean the pedestrian stink of shit, gentlefriends. I speak of the eye-watering perfume of simple mortality. It takes a turn or two to really warm up, but once the gala gets into full swing, it's one not soon forgot.

Before the skin starts to black and the eyes turn to white and the belly bloats like some horrid balloon, it begins. There's a sweetness to it, creeping down your throat and rolling your belly like a butter churn. In truth, I think it speaks to something primal in you. The same part of you mortals that dreads the dark. That *knows,* without a shadow of a doubt, that no matter who you are and what you do, even worms shall have their feasts, and that one turn, you and everything you love will die.

But still, it takes a while for bodies to get so bad you can smell them from miles away. And so when Teardrinker caught a whiff of the high, sweet stink of decay on the Ysiiri whisperwinds, she knew the corpses had to be at least two turns dead.

And that there had to be an awful lot of them.

The woman pulled on her reins, bringing her camel to a stop as she raised her fist to her crew. The driver in the train behind her saw her signal, the long, winding chain of wagons and beasts slowing down, all spit and growls and stomping feet. The heat was brutal—two suns burning the sky a blinding blue and all the desert around them to rippling red. Teardrinker reached for the waterskin on her saddle, took a lukewarm swig as her second pulled up alongside her.

"Trouble?" Cesare asked.

Teardrinker nodded south along the road. "Smells like."

Like all her people, the Dweymeri woman was tall—six foot seven if she was an inch, and every inch of that was muscle. Her skin was deep brown, her features adorned with the intricate facial tattoos worn by all folk of the Dweymeri Isles. A long scar bisected her brow, running over a milk-white left eye and down her cheek. She was dressed like a seafarer: a tricorn hat and some old captain's frock coat. But the oceans she sailed were made of sand now, the only decks she walked were those of her wagon train. After a wreck that killed her entire crew and all her cargo years ago, Teardrinker had decided that the Mother of Oceans hated her guts, arse, and the ship she sailed in on.

So, deserts it was.

The captain shielded her eye against the glare, squinting into the distance. The whisperwinds scratched and clawed about her, the hair on back of her neck tingling. They were still seven turns out of the Hanging Gardens, and it wasn't uncommon for slavers to work this road even in summersdeep. Still, two of three suns were high in the sky, and this close to truelight, she was hoping it'd be too hot for drama.

But the stench was unmistakable.

"Dogger," she hollered. "Graccus, Luka, bring your arms and come with me. Dustwalker, you keep up that ironsong. If a sand kraken ends up chewing on my cunny, I'll be back from the 'byss to chew on *you*."

"Aye, Cap'n!" the big Dweymeri called. Turning to the contraption of iron piping bolted to the rearmost wagon in the train, Dustwalker hefted a large pipe and began beating it like a disobedient hound. The discordant tune of ironsong joined the maddening whispers blowing in off the northern wastes.

"What about me?" Cesare asked.

Teardrinker smirked at her right-hand man. "You're too pretty to risk. Stay here. Keep an eye on the stock."

"They're not doing well in this heat."

The woman nodded. "Water them while you wait. Let them stretch their legs a little. Not too far, though. This is bad country."

"Aye, Cap'n."

Cesare doffed his hat as Dogger, Graccus, and Luka rode up on their camels to join Teardrinker at the front of the line. Each man was dressed in a thick leather jerkin despite the scorch, and Dogger and Graccus were packing heavy crossbows. Luka wielded his slingblades as always, cigarillo hanging from his mouth. The Liisian thought arrows were for cowards, and he was good enough with his slings that she never argued. But how he could stand to smoke in this heat was beyond her.

"Eyes open, mouths shut," Teardrinker ordered. "Let's about it."

The quartet headed down through rocky badlands, the stench growing stronger by the second. Teardrinker's men were as hard a pack of bastards as you'd find under the suns, but even the hardest were born with a sense of smell. Dogger pressed a finger to his nose, blasting a stream of snot from each nostril, cursing by Aa and all four of his daughters. Luka lit another cigarillo, and Teardrinker was tempted to ask him for a puff to rid herself of the taste, accursed heat or no.

They found the wreck about two miles down the road.

It was a short wagon train: two trailers and four camels, all bloating in the sunlight. Teardrinker nodded to her men and they dismounted, wandering through the wreckage with weapons ready. The air was thick with the hymn of tiny wings.

A slaughter, by the look. Arrows littered on the sand and studding the wagon hulls. Teardrinker saw a fallen sword. A broken shield. A long slick of dried blood like a madman's scrawl, and a frantic dance of footprints around a cold cooking pit.

"Slavers," she murmured. "A few turns back."

"Aye," Luka nodded, drawing on his cigarillo. "Looks like."

"Cap'n, I could use a hand over here," Dogger called.

Teardrinker made her way around the fallen beasts, Luka beside her, brushing away the soup of flies. She saw Dogger, crossbow drawn but not raised, his other hand up in supplication. And though he was the kind of fellow whose biggest worry when slitting a man's throat was not getting any on his shoes, the man was speaking gently, as if to a frightened mare.

"Woah, there," he cooed. "Easy, girl . . ."

More blood here, sprayed across the sand, dark brown on deep red. Teardrinker saw the telltale mounds of a dozen freshly dug graves nearby. And looking past Dogger, she saw who it was he spoke at so sweetly.

"Aa's burning cock," she murmured. "Now there's a sight."

A girl. Eighteen at most. Pale skin, burned a little red from the sunlight. Long black hair cut into sharp bangs over dark eyes, her face smudged with dust and dried blood. But Teardrinker could see she was a beauty beneath the mess, high cheekbones and full lips. She held a double-edged gladius, notched from recent use. Her thigh and ribs were wrapped in rags, stained with a different vintage than the blood on her tunic.

"You're a pretty flower," Teardrinker said.

"S-stay away from me," the girl warned.

"Easy," Teardrinker murmured. "You've no need of steel anymore, lass."

"I'll be the judge of that, if it please you," she said, voice shaking.

Luka drifted to the girl's flank, reaching out with a swift hand. But she turned quick as silver, kicked his knee and sent him to the sand. With a gasp, the Liisian found the lass behind him, her gladius poised above the join between his shoulder and neck. His cigarillo dangled from suddenly dust-dry lips.

She's fast.

The girl's eyes flashed as she snarled at Teardrinker.

"Stay away from me, or Four Daughters, I swear I'll end him."

"Dogger, ease off, there's a lad," Teardrinker commanded. "Graccus, put up your crossbow. Give the young dona some room."

Teardrinker watched as her men obeyed, drifting back to let the girl exhale her panic. The woman took a slow step forward, empty hands up and out.

"We've no wish to hurt you, flower. I'm just a trader, and these are just my men. We're traveling to the Hanging Gardens, we smelled the bodies, we came for a look-see. And that's the truth of it. By Mother Trelene, I swear it."

The girl watched the captain with wary eyes. Luka winced as her blade nicked his neck, blood beading on the steel.

"What happened here?" Teardrinker asked, already knowing the answer.

The girl shook her head, tears welling in her lashes.

"Slavers?" Teardrinker asked. "This is bad country for it."

The girl's lip trembled, she tightened her grip on her blade.

"Were you traveling with your family?"

"M-my father," the girl replied.

Teardrinker sized the lass up. She was on the short side, thin, but fit and hard. She'd taken refuge under the wagons, torn down some canvas to shelter from the whisperwinds. Despite the stink, she'd stayed near the wreck where supplies were plentiful and she'd be easier to find, which meant she was smart. And though her hand trembled, she carried that steel like she knew how to swing it. Luka had dropped faster than a bride's unmentionables on her wedding night.

"You're no merchant's daughter," the captain declared.

"My father was a sellsword. He worked the trains out of Nuuvash."

"Where's your da now, Flower?"

"Over there," the girl said, voice cracking. "With th-the others."

Teardrinker looked to the fresh-dug graves. Maybe three feet deep. Dry sand. Desert heat. No wonder the place stank so bad.

"And the slavers?"

"I buried them, too."

"And now you're waiting out here for what?"

The girl glanced in the direction of Dustwalker's ironsong. This far south, there wasn't much risk of sand kraken. But ironsong meant wagons, and wagons meant succor, and staying here with the dead didn't seem to be on her mind, buried da or no.

"I can offer you food," Teardrinker said. "A ride to the Hanging Gardens. And no unwelcome advances from my men. But you're going to have to put down that sword, Flower. Young Luka is our cook as well as a guardsman." Teardrinker risked a small smile. "And as my husband would tell you if he were still among us, you don't want me cooking your supper."

The girl's eyes welled with tears as she glanced to the graves again.

"We'll carve him a stone before we leave," Teardrinker promised softly.

The tears spilled then, the girl's face crumpling as if someone had kicked it in. She let the sword drop, Luka snatching himself loose and rolling up out of the dirt. The girl hung there like a crooked portrait, curtains of blood-matted hair about her face.

The captain almost felt sorry for her.

She approached slowly across the gore-caked earth, shrouded by a halo of flies. And taking off her glove, she extended one callused hand.

"They call me Teardrinker," she said. "Of the Seaspear clan."

The girl reached out with trembling fingers. "M—"

Teardrinker seized the girl's wrist, spun on the spot and flipped her clean over her shoulder. The lass shrieked, crashing onto the dirt. Teardrinker put the boot to her, medium style—just enough to knock what was left of her fight loose from her lungs.

"Dogger, set the irons, there's a lad," the captain said. "Hands and feet."

The Itreyan unslung the manacles from about his waist, bolted them about the girl. She came to her senses, howling and thrashing as Dogger screwed the irons tighter, and Teardrinker drove a boot so hard into her belly she retched into the dirt. The captain let her have another for good measure, just shy of rib-cracking. The girl curled into a ball with a long, breathless moan.

"Get her on her feet," the captain commanded.

Dogger and Graccus dragged the girl up. Teardrinker grabbed a fistful of hair, hauled the girl's head back so she could look into her eyes.

"I promised no untoward advances from my men, and to that I hold. But keep fussing, and I'll hurt you in ways you'll find all manner of unwelcome. You hear me, Flower?"

The girl could only nod, long black hair tangled at the corners of her lips. Teardrinker nodded to Graccus, and the big man dragged the girl around the ruined wagon train, threw her onto the back of his growling camel. Dogger was already looting the wagons, rifling through the barrels and chests. Luka was checking the cut he'd been gifted, glancing at the girl's gladius in the dust.

"You let a slip like that get the drop on you again," Teardrinker warned, "I'll leave you out here for the fucking dustwraiths, you hear me?"

"Aye, Cap'n," he muttered, abashed.

"Help Dogger with the leavings. Bring all the water back to the train. Anything you can carry worth a looting, snag it. Burn the rest."

Teardrinker spat into the dirt, brushed the flies from her good eye as she strode across the blood-caked sand and joined Graccus. She slung herself up onto her camel, and with a sharp kick, the pair were riding back to the wagon train.

Cesare was waiting in the driver's seat, his pretty face sour. He brightened a little when he saw the girl, groaning and half-senseless over the hump of Graccus's beast.

"For me?" he asked. "You shouldn't have, Cap'n."

"Slavers hit a merchant caravan, bit off more than they could chew." Teardrinker nodded to the girl. "She's the only survivor. Graccus and Dogger are bringing back water from the wreckage. See it distributed among the stock."

"Another one died of heatstroke." Cesare motioned back to the train. "Found him when we let the others out to stretch. That's a quarter of our inventory this run."

Teardrinker hauled off her tricorn, dragged her hand along her sweat-drenched scalp. She watched the stock stagger around their cages, men and women and a handful of children, blinking up at the merciless suns. Only a few were in irons—most were so heat-wracked they'd not the strength to run, even if they had somewhere to go. And out here in the Ysiiri Whisperwastes, there was nowhere to get except dead.

"No fear," she said, nodding at the girl. "Look at her. A prize like that will cover our losses and then some. One of the Daughters has smiled on us." She turned to Graccus. "Lock her in with the women. See she's fed a double ration 'til we get to the Gardens. I want her looking ripe on the stocks. You touch her beyond that, I'll cut off your fucking fingers and feed them to you, aye?"

Graccus nodded. "Aye, Cap'n."

"Get the rest back in their cages. Leave the dead one for the restless."

Cesare and Graccus set about it, leaving Teardrinker to brood.

The captain sighed. The third sun would be rising in a few months. This would probably be the last run she'd make until after truelight, and the divinities had been conspiring to fuck it to ruin. An outbreak of bloodflux had wiped out an entire wagon of her stock just a week after they left Rammahd. Young Cisco had got poleaxed when he slipped off for a piss—probably took by a dustwraith, judging by what was left of him. And this heat was threatening to wilt the rest of her crop before it even got to market. All she needed was a cool breeze for a few more turns. Maybe a short spell of rain. She'd sacrificed a strong young calf on the Altar of Storms at Nuuvash before she left. But did Lady Nalipse listen?

After the wreck years ago that had almost ruined her, Teardrinker had vowed to stay away from the water. Running flesh on the seas was a riskier business than driving it on land. But she swore the Mother of Oceans was still trying to make her life a misery, even if it meant getting her sister, the Mother of Storms, in on the torment.

Not a breath of wind.

Not a drop of rain.

Still, that pretty flower was fresh, and curves like hers would fetch a fine price at market. It was a stroke of luck to have found her out here, unspoiled in all this shit. Between the raiders and the slavers and the sand kraken, the Ysiiri Whisperwastes were no place for a girl to roam alone. For Teardrinker to have found her before someone or some*thing* else did, one of the Daughters had to be smiling on her.

It was almost as if someone wanted it this way . . .

The girl was thrown in the frontmost wagon with the other maids and children. The cage was six feet high, rusted iron. The floor was smeared with filth, the reek of sweating bodies and carrion breath almost as bad as the camel corpses had been. The big one named Graccus hadn't been gentle, but true to his captain's word, his hands had done nothing but hurl her down, slam the cage door and twist the lock.

The girl curled up on the floor. Felt the stares of the women about her, the curious eyes of the boys and girls. Her ribs ached from the kicking she'd been gifted, the tears she'd cried cutting tracks down through the blood and dirt on her cheeks. Fighting for calm. Eyes closed. Just breathing.

Finally, she felt gentle hands helping her up. The cage was crowded, but there was room enough for her to sit in a corner, back pressed hard to the bars. She opened her eyes, saw a young, kindly face, smeared with grime, green eyes.

"Do you speak Liisian?" the woman asked.

The girl nodded mutely.

"What's your name?"

The girl whispered through swollen lips. ". . . Mia."

"Four Daughters," the woman tutted, smoothing back the girl's hair. "How did a pretty doll like you end in a place like this?

The girl glanced down at the shadow beneath her.

Up to those glittering green eyes.

"Well," she sighed. "That's the question, isn't it?"

FIREMASS

Four months earlier

King Francisco XV, sovereign ruler of all Itreya, took his place at the edge of the stage. He was decked in a doublet and hose of purest white, cheeks daubed with rose paint. The jewels in his crown sparkled as he spoke, one hand to his chest.

"Ever I sought to rule both wise and just,

But kingly brow as beggar's knees now must;

To kiss the dirt and—"

"Nay!" came a shout.

Tiberius the Elder entered from stage left, surrounded by his Republican conspirators. A silver dagger gleamed in the old man's hand, his jaw set, eyes bright. Without a word, he lunged across the stage, sinking his blade deep into his monarch's chest, once, twice, three times. The audience gasped as bright red blood sprayed, splashing onto the polished boards at their feet. King Francisco clutched his rup-tured heart, sinking to his knees. And with a last groan (a little overcooked, some said afterward), he closed his eyes and died.

Tiberius the Elder held aloft his dagger, delivered his fateful, final lines.

"Heart's blood is spilled, and what shall be, shall be,

No price too steep to stand 'gainst tyranny.

But know, I struck this blow, friends, not for me,

But drenched my blade in name of liberty."

Tiberius looked among the audience, bloody knife in his hands. And as he dropped into a low bow, the curtains closed, heavy red velvet falling across the scene.

The guests cheered as the music swelled, signaling the drama's end. Arkemical chandeliers in the ceiling glowed brighter, banishing the darkness that had accom-panied the final act. Applause rippled across the crowded room, over the mezza-nine above, out to the back of the room. And there, it found a girl, with long raven hair and pale, perfect skin, and a shadow dark enough for three.

Mia Corvere joined in with the guests' applause, though in truth, her eyes had been anywhere except the play. A cool chill flitted across the back of her neck, hidden in the shadows thrown by her hair. Mister Kindly's whisper was velvet soft in her ear.

". . . that was mind-bendingly awful . . . ," *the shadowcat said.*

Mia replied softly, adjusting the ill-fitting masque on her face.

"I thought the chicken blood was a nice touch."

". . . that was thirty minutes of our existence we will never have again, you realize . . ."

"At least they've turned the bloody lights back on."

Letting the crowd clap awhile longer, the curtains finally parted, revealing King Francisco hale and whole, the punctured bladder that had contained his "heart's blood" just visible under his soaked shirt. Joining hands with his murderer, spring-loaded dagger clutched between them, Tiberius the Elder and Francisco XV took a long bow.

"Merry Firemass, gentlefriends!" *the murdered king cried.*

The applause slowly died as the actors left the stage, chatter and laughter re-suming now the play was done. Mia took a sip of her drink, peered around the room. Now the house lights were back up, she could see a little better.

"All right, where is he . . ." *she muttered.*

She'd arrived fashionably late and the ballroom was crowded, but that was no surprise—the soirees of Senator Alexus Aurelius were always popular affairs. With the play concluded, the twelve-piece orchestra took up a bright tune on their gilded mezzanine at the back of the room. Mia watched as marrowborn gentry in crisp frock coats stepped onto the dance floor with graceful dona in their arms, gowns of crimson and silver and gold shimmering in the light of the arkemical chandeliers.

Their faces were hidden behind a dizzying array of masques, a hundred different shapes and themes. Mia could see square-faced voltos *and laughing* punchinellos *and half-cut* dominos, *bejeweled paint and gleaming ivory and fans of peacock feathers. The most common design among the salon crowd was the triple-sun of Aa, or beautiful variants of the Face of Tsana. It was Firemass, after all, and most folk at least tried to make some attempt to venerate the Everseeing and his firstborn daughter before the inevitable hedonism of the feasteve got into full swing.**

Mia was clad in an off-the-shoulder gown of blood-red, layers of Liisian silk flowing to the floor. Her half-cut corset was cinched tight, a string of dark rubies spilling into her cleavage, and while she appreciated the effect the corset and jewels had of emphasizing her assets, the admiring glances she'd been getting all nevernight didn't make it any easier to bloody breathe. Her own features were covered by a Face of Tsana—a masque depicting the warrior-goddess's helm, a plume of firebird feathers about the edge. Her lips and chin were bare, which made it a little easier to drink. And smoke. And swear.

"'Byss and fucking blood, where is he?" she muttered, eyes roaming the crowd.

She felt that chill again, the soft whisper in her ear.

"... the booths ...," Mister Kindly said.

Mia looked over the swaying throng to the walls above the dance floor. Senator Aurelius's ballroom had been built like an amphitheater, with the stage at one end, seats arranged in concentric rings, and smaller private booths overlooking the main floor. Through the smoke and long sheaves of sheer silk strung from the ceiling, she finally saw a tall young man, decked in a long white frock coat and black cravat, the twin horses of his familia embroidered in golden thread upon his breast.

---

*Firemass is a celebration that marks the turn toward summersdeep in the Itreyan calendar. Dedicated to Tsana, the Lady of Fire, it falls on the eighth month before truelight—the holiest of Aa's feasts, when all three suns burn in the sky.

Tsana is Aa's firstborn daughter, a virgin goddess who serves as patron of both warriors and women. Firemass is marked by a four-hour cathedral mass, and is meant to be a turn of reflection and chaste contemplation. Of course, most of the Republic's citizenry use it as an excuse to don masques and hold a raucous piss-up, indulging in precisely the kind of behavior Tsana frowns upon.

But, as with spouses, so with goddesses, gentlefriends; it is often better to beg forgiveness than seek permission.

". . . gaius aurelius . . ."

Mia lifted her ivory cigarillo holder, took a thoughtful drag. The young man's face was half-hidden behind a golden domino *with a triple-sun motif, but she could see a strong jawline and a handsome smile as he whispered into the ear of a beautiful young woman in a stylish gown beside him.*

"Looks like he's made a friend," *Mia whispered, gray spilling from her lips.*

". . . well, he *is* a senator's son. he is unlikely to spend the nevernight alone . . ."

"Not if I can help it. Eclipse, go tell Dove to be ready. We may need to leave in a hurry."

A soft growl came from the shadows beneath her dress.

". . . DOVE IS AN IDIOT . . ."

"All the more reason to make sure he's awake. I think I'll go say hello to our esteemed senator's firstborn. And his friend."

". . . two is company, mia . . . ," *Mister Kindly warned.*

"True enough. But there's plenty of fun to be had in a crowd."

Slipping from her corner, Mia drifted through the ballroom like the smoke from her lips. Smiling at the compliments, politely declining entreaties to dance. She strode blithely past two guards in fine-cut coats at the bottom of the stairs, pretending she belonged and thus, appearing to do just that. There was no one else in the room who shouldn't have been there, after all. The invitation had taken her five patient nevernights to steal from the house of Dona Grigorio.* And the masques these marrowborn fools insisted on wearing every feasteve made it easy to walk among them unmarked. Especially with her curves strangled in a fashion designed to draw the eye away from her face.

Mia checked her paint in a small silver mirror case, applied another dark red coat to her lips. And taking one last drag from her cigarillo, she crushed it under her boot heel and stumbled past the velvet curtains into Aurelius's booth.

"O, apologies," *she said.*

Don Aurelius and his companion looked up in mild surprise. The pair were

---

*The three drams of the toxin known as "Mishap" that Mia had slipped into the dona's tea yestereve ensured she'd not be up to attending Senator Aurelius's soiree—suffering explosive discharge from every orifice does tend to put a damper on one's ability to hobnob. Mia normally would have used a smaller dose, especially on someone so elderly. But in the five turns she'd been casing Grigorio's palazzo, the old woman had proved herself to be a battleaxe of the first order, whose only pleasure seemed to be shouting at a portrait of her dead husband and beating her slaves. So, Mia found it hard to feel too guilty about giving the old bitch an extra-large serving.

Though she did feel sorry for whoever had to clean up the mess afterward.

sat on a long divan of crushed velvet, half-empty glasses and a bottle of fine Vaanian red on the table before them. Mia pressed her hand to her breast in faux alarm.

"I thought this one empty. Forgiveness, I beg you."

The young don gave a small nod. His handsome smile was dark with wine. "Think nothing of it, Mi Dona."

"Do you . . ." Mia heaved a sigh, uncertain. Reaching up, she unfastened her masque, used it to fan her face. "Apologies, might I trouble you to sit for a moment? It's hotter than truelight in here, and this dress makes it frightfully hard to breathe."

Aurelius ran his eyes over Mia's unmasqued features. The black eyes framed with artful smudges of kohl. The milk-pale skin and pouting, dark red lips, the necklet of jewels at her slender throat, a fox-quick glance to the bare skin below as Mia made a show of adjusting her corsetry.

"By all means, Mi Dona," he smiled, motioning to the spare divan.

"Aa bless," Mia said, sinking down onto the velvet, fanning herself again.

"Allow me to introduce myself. I am Don Gaius Neraus Aurelius, and my lovely accomplice here is Alenna Bosconi."

Aurelius's companion was a Liisian beauty around Mia's age—probably the daughter of local administratii, by the look. Dark of hair and iris, her skin olive, the gold chiffon of her gown accented by metallic powder on her lips and lashes.

"Four Daughters, I adore your dress," Mia gasped. "Is it an Albretto?"

"A fine eye," Alenna replied, raising her glass. "My compliments."

"I've a fitting with her next week," Mia said. "Presuming my aunt lets me out of the palazzo again. I've a suspicion she'll have me sent to a convent amorrow."

"Who is your aunt, Mi Dona?" Aurelius asked.

"Dona Grigorio. Stuffy old cow." Mia pointed to the wine. "May I?"

Aurelius watched her fill a glass and finish it just as swift, bemusement in his eye. "Forgive me, I didn't know the dona had a niece?"

"Color me distinctly unsurprised, Mi Don," Mia sighed. "I've been in Galante almost a month and she doesn't let me out of the palazzo. I had to sneak out to be here this eve. Father sent me to summer with her, insisting she'd teach me how to behave like a god-fearing daughter of Aa should."

"Meaning you don't behave like one should now?" Aurelius smiled.

Mia made a face. "Honestly, you'd think I'd bedded one of the stableboys, the way he goes on about it."

Aurelius raised the bottle to Mia's glass with an inquiring tilt of his head.

"Another?"

"Most generous, sir."

Aurelius poured, passed the full glass. Mia took it with a knowing smile, let her fingertips brush the young don's wrist, arkemical current prickling between their skin. Alenna raised her glass to golden lips, faint annoyance in her voice.

"There's not much left, Gaius," she warned, glancing at the bottle.

Mia looked to the girl, tucking a stray lock of hair behind her ear. Any fear she might have felt was swallowed by the shadows at her feet. She rose from her seat with silken grace, sank down on the divan beside the golden beauty. Looking into Alenna's eyes, she took a small sip of the wine. It was rich, velvet smooth, dancing dark upon her tongue. And taking away her empty glass, Mia pressed her own into Alenna's hand, fingers entwined, lifting it to those golden lips.

She looked over her shoulder to Aurelius, saw him watching, enraptured. She smiled as she whispered, loud enough to be heard over the music below.

"I don't mind sharing."

*A*urelius stood behind her, hands roaming her bare arms, across her breasts. Mia felt his lips at her ear, brush the edge of her jaw, reaching back to tangle her fingers in his hair. Leaning into the hardness at his crotch she sought his mouth, sighing as he left a trail of burning kisses down her throat, stubble tickling her skin. Finding the silken ribbon lacing the back of her corset, he pulled it loose with slow, steady hands.

Alenna was behind him, unbuttoning his jacket and letting it fall to the floor. Her cheeks were flushed from more than drink, long fingernails tearing his silken shirt and leaving his torso bare. Mia reached back to the hardness of his chest, fingers slipping down the troughs and furrows of his abdomen. His lips were at the nape of her neck, she felt the press of his teeth, sighing yes as he bit harder, seeking his mouth again. But with his free hand, he took hold of her long tresses, easing her head back, back, goosebumps thrilling along her skin as he pulled her corset away.

The music was faint and far above, near lost beneath the song of their sighs. They'd stumbled down the stairs, Aurelius ushering Mia and Alenna before him with playful slaps on their backsides. House guards pretended to pay no mind as the trio had stumbled past, Mia pressing her lips to Aurelius's throat as he'd stopped to give the Liisian beauty a long kiss. He'd pushed Mia against the wall and reached between her legs, setting to work with clever fingers right there in the hallway. They'd barely made it to his room.

Like most marrowborn palazzos, the bedchambers were underground—all the better to shield them from the suns' relentless light. The air was cooler down here, *the light from the arkemical globes low and smoky. Mia's corset fell to the floor-boards as Aurelius slipped his hand inside her gown. She sighed as she felt his hands cupping her breasts, pinching one swollen nipple hard enough to make her gasp. He peeled her dress off, letting it fall in a rumpled heap about her ankles. She sought his belt, found Alenna's hands there also, their fingers entwined as they worked the buckle loose. Mia felt Aurelius's hands roam lower, arkemical current dancing on her skin as his fingers slipped over her belly, down through her soft curls to her aching lips beyond.*

She groaned as his fingers went to work, weakening her knees. Turning her head, she sought his mouth with her own, but his grip on her hair pulled her up short, left her gasping, moaning as she pushed her arse back, grinding against his crotch with the same rhythm he was strumming on her.

His belt finally loose, the beauty tore the buttons on his britches free, Mia's fingers slipping inside. She found her mark after a moment, smiling at his groan as she took his heat in her hand. She felt Alenna's hands also, the pair of them working his length as his finger slipped inside her, stars bursting behind her eyes, almost bringing her legs out from under her.

Aurelius turned, his mouth finding Alenna's, their tongues entwined. Mia un-tangled his hand from her hair, curled her fingers in his own, desperate to kiss him. But her skin prickled as she sensed him step aside, as she felt warm lips on her shoulder, the back of her neck, warm hands slipping about her waist.

Not his . . .

Alenna's fingertips were dancing up her arms, flitting across the swell of her breasts. Her breath came quicker as she felt the girl's hand at her chin, turning her slow. Heart hammering, Mia came about to face her.

The girl was beautiful, bee-stung lips parted, dark eyes welling with desire in the smoky light. Her chest was heaving as she pressed closer, still clothed against Mia's near-naked body. Aurelius began kissing the nape of Alenna's neck as she smoothed back a lock of long dark hair from Mia's cheek, Mia feeling a thrill run all the way to her toes as the beauty leaned in to kiss her. Close. Closer. Clos—

"No," *Mia said, pulling away.*

Alenna's eyes clouded with confusion, and she glanced over her shoulder to Aurelius. The young don quirked an eyebrow in question.

"Not on the mouth," *Mia said.*

The beauty's golden lips curled in a knowing smile. Dark eyes roamed Mia's naked body, drinking her in.

"Everywhere else, then," *she breathed.*

Alenna ran her hands down Mia's cheeks, the jewels at her throat, making her shiver. And slow as agony, she leaned in and pressed her lips to Mia's neck.

Mia sighed, goosebumps prickling, no fear inside her. Leaning her head back, surrendering, eyelashes fluttering as Alenna's hands cupped her heaving breasts, floating over her hips, caressing her arse. Mia couldn't feel anything but those hands, those lips, teeth nipping, breath warm on her skin, the beauty's mouth roaming down to the swell of her breast. She groaned as the girl took her nipple into her mouth, tongue flickering over the swollen tip, all the room spinning.

Alenna's fingernails sent shivers up Mia's spine as they skimmed her skin, guiding her backward. She felt the bedframe behind her knees, bending like a sapling before the storm and tumbling back with a gasp onto the furs.

Alenna sighed as Aurelius nuzzled her neck from behind, working the ties of her corset loose. Slipping her dress off her shoulders, the young don let the golden chiffon tumble away in a shimmering wave, underthings following, stripping her bare.

Mia's eyes roamed the girl's body as she climbed onto the bed on hands and knees, prowling like a cat. Alenna knelt above her, sighing as the young don sank to his knees behind her, kisses trailing down her back, over her arse. Mia felt the girl's hands trail the insides of her shivering thighs, breath coming fast as those fingers brushed her lips. Alenna was breathing quick too, groaning as Aurelius pressed his mouth between her legs, went to work with his tongue. Her eyes were bright with lust as she leaned in close, seeking Mia's mouth again.

Mia turned away, one hand to the girl's lips.

"No."

She reached out across Alenna's skin, finding Aurelius's hand at the girl's hip. Entwining her fingers with his own, the beauty sighed in protest as Mia dragged him away from his prize. Eyes on his. Breathless.

"Kiss me," she begged.

Aurelius smiled as Alenna descended, the girl's kisses like ice and fire across Mia's throat, breasts, belly. The young don crawled up the mattress as the girl sank farther down, licking the cusp of Mia's navel, the divots at her hips. Mia felt gentle teeth on the inside of her thighs, hands roaming her skin, whimpering as Alenna blew on her softly, lips just a whisper away from her own. Mia reached up with one hand, down with the other, tangling her fingers in their hair. She dragged Aurelius toward her, pleading, pulling Alenna in. And the don's mouth closed over her own, smothering her breathless moan as she felt the first touch of the beauty's tongue.

They went to work, the pair of them, Mia writhing on the fur as they adored her. A heat like she'd never known burned between her legs as Alenna kissed her like no man ever had, back arching, fingers knotted in the girl's tresses. She could taste the girl on Aurelius's tongue, the salt and sweetness of it. She kissed him fiercely, biting his lip hard enough to split the skin, dark red paint mixing with the blood on their mouths. Her lips smothered his gasp of pain, her tongue found his, teasing, tasting, dancing in some pale semblance of the beauty's between her legs.

Time stopped turning, the world stopped spinning. Breaking away from her mouth, the don left a trail of bloody kisses down her neck. Mia gasped as he descended, licking, suckling, biting, eyes fluttering closed as Alenna began her work in earnest, lapping at her swollen bud.

Aurelius lifted his head.

A quick shudder ran through him.

A soft groan slipped past his lips.

And drawing in a ragged breath, the young don coughed a mouthful of bright red blood all over Mia's breasts.

"F-four Daughters . . ."

Aurelius stared in horror at the scarlet on Mia's skin, on his hands. Mia pulled herself up on her elbows as he fell back with another red cough, fingers at his throat. Alenna realized what was happening, her face spattered with crimson. Rearing back, she drew breath to scream as Mia lunged across the bed and seized her throat, dragging her into a choke hold.

"Hushhh, now," she whispered, lips brushing the beauty's ear.

The girl struggled in Mia's grip, but the assassin was stronger, harder. The pair toppled to the floorboards, into the tangle of their clothes as Aurelius began thrashing, fingernails clawing his neck as he coughed up another lungful.

"I know it's hard to watch," Mia whispered to the beauty. "But it only lasts a moment."

"Th-the wine . . . ?"

Mia shook her head. "Not on the mouth, remember?"

Alenna stared at the split Mia had bitten in Aurelius's lip, the red paint smeared with the blood around his mouth. The young don flopped on the bed like a landed fish, every muscle seizing tight, face twisted. Alenna's lips parted to scream as a shadow moved on the headboard, another at the foot—two shapes cut from the darkness itself. Mia's hand closed about the girl's mouth again as Mister Kindly and Eclipse coalesced, staring enraptured as the young don groaned in agony, blood bubbling between his teeth. And with eyes wide, lips peeling back in a silent cry, the first and only son of Senator Alexus Aurelius exhaled his final breath.

"Hear me, Niah," Mia whispered. "Hear me, Mother. This flesh your feast. This blood your wine. This life, this end, my gift to you. Hold him close."

Mister Kindly tilted his head, watching the young don die.
His purr almost sounded like a sigh.

Mia was thirsty.

That was the worst part. The cage, the heat, the stink, she could stomach it all. But no matter how much her captors gave her to drink, in this bastard desert it was never enough. When Dogger or Graccus shoved the ladle through the bars of her cage, that lukewarm water seemed a gift from the Mother herself. But between the swelter and the sweat and the wagon's crush, her lips were soon cracking, her tongue swollen and dry.

The captives were jammed together like strips of salt pork in a barrel, and the smell was sickening. The first turn she'd spent baking inside that kiln-hot cage, Mia had begun to think she'd made an awful mistake.

Think it. But not fear it.

Never flinch.

Never fear.

Mia tried not to talk much. She didn't want to grow too close to the other captives, knowing what was coming at the Hanging Gardens. But she watched how they cared for each other, an elderly woman comforting a lass crying for her mother, or a girl giving her own meager ration to a boy who'd puked his own meal down the front of his rags. Little kindnesses that spoke of the biggest hearts.

Mia wondered where her own might be.

No place for it out here, girl.

Her captors were a motley bunch. Their captain, Teardrinker, looked to be bedding her second, Cesare, though Mia had no doubt who'd be holding the reins on that particular ride. No woman got to lead an outfit of cutthroat slavers in the Ysiiri wastes unless she had the sharpest of teeth.

The Itreyans, Dogger and Graccus, both seemed the typical brand of bastard you'd find in any one of a hundred fleshpeddler outfits operating out of Ysiir. As per Captain's orders, they didn't lay a finger on the women. But from the hungry looks they threw her way, Mia imagined they resented it no end. They spent their downtime playing Spank with a dog-eared set of playing cards, betting with a handful of clipped beggars.*

---

*You'll remember the coinage of Itreya is nicknamed for the folks most often found handling them, gentlefriends. Coppers are called "beggars." Silvers are called "priests." Depending on the social standing of the person you ask, gold coins are either called

The big Dweymeri, Dustwalker, seemed a more careful sort. He played the flute, and he'd treat the captives to a melody when he had no other work to do. The last of them was Luka—the young Liisian Mia had kicked into the dust. Short locks and a dimpled smile. The slop he cooked tasted worse than a pig's arsehole, but Mia had seen him sneak some extra bread to the children at evemeal.

And that was it. Six leather-clad slavers and a row of locked iron bars between her and the freedom any of the captives around her would have killed to taste. All was sweat and puke. Shit and blood. At least half the women in her wagon cried themselves to what little sleep they could find. But not Mia Corvere.

The girl sat against the door and waited. Ragged bangs hanging in deep, dark eyes. The reek of sweat and filth was inescapable, the press of the bodies around her enough to make her ill. But she swallowed her vomit along with her pride, pissing in the road when commanded and keeping her mouth on the right side of shut. And if the shadow pooled beneath her was too dark—dark enough for two, perhaps—then the covered wagon's innards were too gloomy to notice.

It was only four more turns to the Hanging Gardens. Four more turns of this awful heat, this godless stink, this sickening, trundling sway. Four more turns.

Patience, she'd tell herself, whispering the word like a prayer.

If Vengeance has a mother, her name is Patience.

It was maybe an hour 'til nevernight's end, and the caravan was pulling over to the side of its long, dusty road. Peering out through the tear in the wagon's canopy, Mia could see a tumble of sandstone bluffs throwing shadows on the desert sand. It was an obvious—and therefore, dangerous—spot to shelter, but best to stop here in shade than press on for another hour and spend the entire turn baking in the suns.

Mia heard Dustwalker in the supply wagon as always, banging out an occasional peal of ironsong to scare off any sand kraken daring enough to travel this far south.* She caught a glimpse of Graccus, scouting the rocky

---

"tossers" or "get away from me you filthy pleb before I have my man here break your fucking legs."

*Typically, the predators of the Ysiiri Whisperwastes don't travel much past the Great Salt, and the biggest sand kraken are only found in the deep deserts. Occasionally, smaller specimens will range south when game grows scarce, and in recent years, several enterprising outfits operating out of southern Ysiir have set about capturing

outcroppings from atop his snarling, shit-machine of a camel. He looked salty, face dripping as he squinted up at the suns and cursed the Everseeing for a bastard.

The first arrow took him in the chest.

It whizzed out of the sunlight, piercing his jerkin with a thud. A stupid frown darkened Graccus's brow, but the next two arrows flying out of the rocks wiped it off his face, sent him tumbling backward off his beast in a spray of bright red.

"Raiders!" Teardrinker bellowed.

The women in Mia's wagon screamed as a hail of arrows rained down on the caravan, punching through the canopy. Mia heard a gasp, felt the flesh around her shift. A young lass sank down in the crush, an arrow in her eye. One of the sprats took a shaft to the leg, started howling, the entire mass of bodies around her shifting like the sea in a storm and crushing her against the bars.

"'Byss and blood . . ."

Mia heard galloping hooves, the sound of black-feathered rain. Somewhere distant, Dustwalker was roaring in pain, Teardrinker shouting orders. The ring of steel rose over the bellow of wounded camels, the hiss of spraying sand. Mia cursed again as she was shoved face-first against the bars, the folk around her boiling to a panic.

"Right, fuck this," she spat.

Reaching down to her boot, Mia twisted the heel, retrieving her trusty lockpicks. In a moment, she was free of her manacles, reaching between the rusted bars. She set to sweet-talking the lock, tongue poking out in concentration. An arrow sheared through the canopy just shy of her head, another thudded into the wood near her hand.

"*. . . you may wish to hurry . . .*"

The whisper was soft as baby's breath, intended for her ears only.

"You're not helping," she whispered back.

"*. . . i am offering moral support . . .*"

"You're being an annoying little shit."

"*. . . that too . . .*"

---

these roaming kraken, selling them for use in spectacle matches during the *Venatus Magni*—the great games held in honor of Aa during the Feast of Truelight.

The masters of the *venatus* are constantly looking for ways to outdo the spectacle (and attendance) of previous games, and if the thought of watching a favorite gladiatii battling a horror from the Ysiiri Whisperwastes doesn't get arses on seats, very little will, gentlefriends.

The lock sprung open in her hand and Mia kicked the door aside, tumbled out in the blazing light. She rolled beneath the wagon as the other women realized their cage was open, falling over themselves in their bid to escape.

Mia could see a half-dozen raiders circling the caravan. They were clad in dark leather and desert colors, a mix of sexes and skin tones. Cesare was dead, punctured with black-feathered arrows. Mia saw no sign of Luka, but Dogger was crouched behind the aft wagon, Dustwalker's corpse beside him. Teardrinker's camel had taken an arrow to the throat, and the captain was hunkered behind its body, crossbow in hand.

"Stinking whoresons!" she roared. "Do you know who I am?"

The riders only jeered in response. Riding in that incessant circle, driving the escaping women back toward the wagons, and the captives in the other cages into a frothing panic.

"Diversion," Mia realized.

"*. . . from what . . . ?*"

Dogger ducked out from cover, loosing a quick shot with his crossbow. From somewhere among the rocks, a black-feathered arrow flashed, striking him in the chest. Dogger fell, scarlet bubbles bursting on his lips.

"From that sharpshooter up there," Mia muttered.

The girl reached out to the shadows beneath the wagon, gathering them up like a seamstress pulling thread. It was so bright out here, so different from the belly of the Quiet Mountain. But ever so slowly, she stitched the shadows together, weaving them into a cloak. And beneath it, she became little more than a smudge, like a greasy fingerprint on a portrait of the world.

Of course, she could barely see a bloody thing. She'd always thought it cruel that the Goddess of Night would give her the gift to remain unseen but make her almost blind while doing it. Still, blind was better than butchered.

Mia crept closer to the wheel, moving by feel, preparing to dash from cover.

"*. . . try not to get shot . . .*"

"That's excellent advice, Mister Kindly. My thanks."

"*. . . moral support, as i said . . .*"

Then she was moving. Crouched low, hands out before her, away from the wagons and toward the outcropping ahead. All the world was a blur, coffee black and milky white. The dark shape of a horse and rider loomed out of the nothingness, clipped her hard as it rode by. She staggered, wobbling blind until she hit a low outcropping of rock with her shins and tumbled into cover with a curse.

"Ow, fuck it."

"*. . . o, poor child, where does it hurt . . . ?*"

The girl pulled herself up with a wince, slapped her rump.

"Kiss it better?"

"*. . . perhaps a bath is in order first . . .*"

The girl was off again, groping her way up the rocky slope, moving by feel and sound alone. She could still hear Teardrinker roaring challenge, but the girl was listening for the telltale hiss of arrows, the whip-snap of a bowstring. And there it came . . . and there again, Mia circling up and around, quiet as a particularly quiet dormouse who'd just been appointed Master of Quiet at the Iron Collegium.*

Another arrow. Another snap of the bowstring. Mia could hear soft whispering between each shot, wondering if there was more than one shooter up there. She was behind them now, hidden among a tumble of boulders. And throwing aside her shadows, she peered over her cover to find out how many bowmen she'd have to murder.

Turned out, there was none at all.

O, there was an archer, no doubt. But she was no more a bowman than Mia was a swordsman. A woman, clad in gray leathers and mottled brown, her blond hair cropped short. Whenever a shot presented itself, she'd press an arrow to her lips, whisper a prayer, then let fly. Whatever divinity she prayed to seemed to be listening, too—as Luka dashed for one of the camels, the archer put an arrow in his shoulder, another in his shin as he scrambled back into cover.

The rock crushed her head with the first blow, but Mia smashed it twice more into the back of her skull, just to be sure. The archer fell with a bubbling gurgle, fingers twitching. And picking up her bow, Mia drew the string to her lips, took aim, and put a black-feathered arrow into the spine of one of the raiders below.

The woman twisted in her saddle, fell with a bloody cry. A comrade saw her fall, turned to the bluffs above and tumbled back off his horse with an arrow in his throat. Another raider cried warning, "*'Ware the rocks! The rocks!*" as Mia's shot took him in the thigh, her second in his belly. A slingblade glit-

---

*You may recall the Ironpriests of the Collegium have their tongues removed at a young age to preserve the secrets of their order. Technically, there is no "Master of Quiet" at the Collegium—that was simply puffery on my part. But I was concerned you wouldn't get the joke otherwise.

. . . o, never mind.

Bastards.

What do you know about funny anyway?

tered as it flew out from the cover of the middle wagon, near taking the man's head off his shoulders.

The raiders were all a confusion now, their sharpshooter gone, and their plan along with her. Teardrinker took a shot with her crossbow, killing a horse and sending its rider to the dirt. Mia killed another rider with two shots to the chest. The last few raiders broke, scooping up their horseless comrade and galloping away as fast as their steeds could take them.

"... *fine shooting* ..."

Mia looked to the shadow sitting atop the archer's corpse. It was small, wore the shape of a cat, cleaning a semitranslucent paw with a semitranslucent tongue.

"My thanks," Mia bowed.

"... *that was sarcasm* ...," Mister Kindly replied. "... *you let four of them get away* ..."

Mia made a face, raised the knuckles at the shadowcat.

"... *while we're still alone, i should probably take this opportunity to point out the insanity of this scheme of yours again* ..."

"O, aye, Daughters forbid you let a turn pass without riding my arse about it."

Mia wiped her bloody hand on the dead archer's britches, slung her quiver of arrows over her shoulder. And bow in hand, she made her way carefully down the slope to the carnage around the 'van.

The women captives were still huddled around their cage. Graccus, Dogger, Dustwalker and Cesare were all dead. Luka was slumped near the middle wagon, arrows in his shoulder and shin. Mia watched him try to get to his feet, settling instead for one knee. His eyes were locked on hers, his second slingblade in hand.

Teardrinker had taken an arrow to the leg somewhere in the fray. Her face was spattered with blood, but she still aimed her crossbow with steady hands right at Mia. The girl stopped forty feet away, raised her bow. It was finely crafted—horn and ash, graven with prayers to the Lady of Storms. It'd put an arrow through an iron breastplate at this range. And Captain Teardrinker was wearing nothing close to iron.

"That father of yours taught you well, girl," the captain called. "Fine shooting."

"... *pfft* ...," whispered her shadow.

Mia kicked the dark pooled around her feet, hissing for silence.

"I've no wish to kill you, Captain," Mia called.

"Well there's a stroke of fortune. I've no wish to fucking die, either."

The captain looked at the corpses around her, the wreckage of her crew, the arrow in her leg, down the long road to the Hanging Gardens.

"I suppose we could call this even," she called. "I was planning on fetching a fine price for you at market, but saving my life seems fair tithe. What say you ride up front with me for the rest of the trip, see us safe to the Gardens? I can cut you in on some of the profit? Twenty percent?"

Mia shook her head. "I don't want that, either."

"Well, what *do* you want?" Teardrinker spat, stare locked on the bow in Mia's grip. "You're holding decent cards, girl. You get a say in how this hand is played."

Mia looked to the other women huddled around the forewagon. They were filthy and haggard, clad in little more than rags. The dusty road stretched out across the blood-red sand, and she knew full well the fate that awaited them at the end of it.

"I want back in the cage," Mia said.

Teardrinker blinked. "You just broke out of the cage . . ."

"I chose you very carefully, Captain. Your reputation is well known. You don't let your men spoil your goods. And you have an accord with the Lions of Leonides, neh?"

"Leonides?" Exasperation crept into Teardrinker's voice. "What in the name of Aa's burning cock does a gladiatii stable have to do with any of this?"

"Well, that's the rub, isn't it?"

The girl lowered her bow with a small smile.

"I want you to sell me to them."

CHAPTER 3

SHADOWS

Mia lay naked on the floor, spattered in red, Alenna in her arms. Music still swelled faintly from the ball upstairs, none of the senator's guests any the wiser that his only son had been murdered right below their heels. Mister Kindly sat on the headboard, staring at the young don's corpse. Eclipse licked her lips with a translucent tongue, the shadowwolf's sigh rumbling through the floor.

The girl in Mia's arms shivered at the sight of them.

"I'm going to take my hand away now, love," Mia whispered. *"I'm not going to hurt you. I'm going to tie you up, put my clothes back on, and then slip out into the sunlight and you're never going to see me again. Does that sound fair?"*

Alenna nodded frantically, blinking the tears from her eyes.

Eclipse's soft feminine voice seemed to come from below the floorboards.

". . . THAT IS FOOLISH . . ."

". . . and you would be the expert on foolishness, pup . . . ," *Mister Kindly sneered.*

". . . BETTER TO BE RID OF HER. WE HAVE NO REASON TO LET HER LIVE . . ."

"And no reason to end her," Mia replied. *"Unless someone is paying me. Now, shouldn't one of you be watching the hallway in case a guard comes down here?"*

". . . i kept watch last time, when you ended that magistrate . . ."

". . . LIAR, I KEPT WATCH OUTSIDE THE WHOLE TIME. YOU WERE FEEDING LIKE A SOW AT TROUGH . . ."

". . . and how would you know that, if you were keeping watch outside the whole time . . . ?"

"If you two are quite finished? I give less than no fucks for who does it, but one of you better get out there, because someone's go—"

A soft knock sounded at the door. A deep voice calling beyond.

"Mi Don?"

Mia cursed beneath her breath, grip tightening on Alenna's throat.

"Mi Don," said a second voice. *"Your father requests your presence."*

Guards, by the sound. At least two of them . . .

". . . IT WAS YOUR TURN . . . ," *Eclipse whispered fierce.*

". . . lying mongr— . . ."

Mia hissed for silence, her mind racing. With guards outside the bedchamber door, her chances of slipping out unnoticed were aflame. Dove was waiting with the carriage upstairs, but he wouldn't be any use to her down here. She could fight easily enough, but she was buck naked, all but unarmed, and the noise would only bring more guards. The shadows down here were deep, but with the bedchambers in the basements, there weren't any windows for her to climb out o—

Mia gasped as Alenna's elbow collided with her ribs, and with a black curse, the girl cracked her head back into Mia's nose. Her grip momentarily loosened, Alenna drew breath and screamed, only partially muffled by Mia's fingers.

"Murder!" she cried. *"Help me!"*

Mia slammed her fist into the side of the girl's head, once, twice, knocking her senseless. She heard a curse, a heavy thump as something crashed into the door.

"Mi Don?" someone shouted. *"Open up!"*

". . . it was your turn . . ."

". . . LIAR . . ."

"Will the pair of you shut up!"

Mia slung her dress over her head as the door shuddered on its hinges. Fishing about in her abandoned corset, she retrieved her gravebone dagger, the crow on the hilt rebuking her with its glittering amber stare. And reaching to the shadows around her, she dragged them over her head, throwing all the world into black and disappearing utterly beneath it.

The door crashed open, two blurred shapes silhouetted against the light. One of them cried Aurelius's name, moving in what Mia hoped was the direction of the bed. The other saw the naked, blood-spattered Liisian girl on the floor and crouched beside her. And with the door now clear, Mia slung aside her cloak of shadows and ran.

The guards bellowed for her to stop, but Mia paid no mind, sprinting down the plush hallway toward the broad stairs. Two more guards appeared above, frowning in confusion at the bloodstained girl barreling up the stairs toward them. One held up a hand to stop her as Mia's dagger flashed, in and out, hilt-deep in his belly. The man gasped and fell, tumbling down the stairs as his comrade cried warning, hefting his shortsword. Mia twisted sideways, gasping as his blade cut deep into her shoulder and upper arm, her whistling counterstrike slicing his neck clean through.

The man collapsed, gargling, and Mia was already gone, up out of the stair-well and onto the ground floor. She burst into the main hall, the marrowborn dons and donas crying out in alarm at the sight of her—bloodied blade in one hand, dark hair strewn around darker eyes, wide with fury.

"Pardon me, Mi Dona," she begged, smashing some pretty young thing aside as she tore through the hall. More guards burst into the room, unsure who to chase or why. The pair from Aurelius's bedchamber appeared at the top of the stairs, scanning the confused crowd, finally spotting Mia as she pushed her way through the mob.

"The girl in red!" one bellowed. "Stop her!"

"Assassin!" the other cried. "The senator's son, slain!"

The hall dissolved into chaos, some folk reaching for Mia, others fleeing before her. She cut some well-heeled administratii from thigh to crotch as he made a grab for her, elbowed another gent in the face and dropped him cold. The knife in her hand and the look in her eye dissuaded the other do-gooders in the crowd, and with a sidestep, a shove, and a rolling tumble, she was through the double doors, sprinting down the plush entry hall. Snatching a tumbler off the drinks tray of a gob-smacked servant, she belted down the goldwine inside before hurling it at the guard rushing at her, bouncing the heavy crystal off his head and sending him sprawling.

Bursting through the doors, out into the courtyard outside Aurelius's palazzo. The cries of "Assassin!" echoed behind her, three guards rushing up the stairs to meet her, the twin suns in her eyes almost blinding.

"Shit . . ."

The guards each had a short, double-edged gladius and a murderous stare. Her shoulder was bleeding freely, her gown soaked with blood. Mia was forced into defense; reaching out to the leader's shadow and fixing his boots to the floor, rolling past their blades, kicking out at a pair of legs as she tumbled, scrambling to her feet. She dashed toward the horses and carriages parked around Aurelius's front yard, spying one amid the crowd.

"Dove!" she roared.

A teenaged boy among the throng raised his head. He was dressed in a simple rectangular volto masque, servant's finery, dark hair cropped short. A cigarillo hung from one corner of his mouth. Three bloody tears crawled down his masque's right cheek. He didn't much look the part of a Hand in the Church of Our Lady of Blessed Murder, but at the sound of Mia's second cry, he stood suddenly in the driver's seat.

"All right?" he called.

"Do I look all-fucking-right?" Mia shouted, sprinting toward him.

Mia's Hand took in the sight of his wounded Blade, the guards on her tail. Spitting out his cigarillo, the boy reached into his greatcoat and produced two small crossbows. Taking careful aim, he felled the guards closest to Mia with two swift shots.

"Run!" he called, beckoning.

"O, aye, you reckon?"

A whistling sound by Mia's ear told her more guards had arrived with crossbows of their own, and as she barreled past the astonished coach drivers, a burst of white hot pain in her backside told her at least one of them was a halfway decent shot.

She stumbled, falling with a curse and grating her palms and knees like cheese on the flagstones. Hissing in pain, she scrambled back to her feet, clutching the crossbow bolt protruding from her backside.

"Maw's teeth, did they just shoot you in th—"

"Just shoot them back, you fucking nonce!"

Dove fired again, dropping another guard with a quarrel in his throat. The boy ducked to reload, and a flurry of quarrels flew over Mia's head, perforating *two of the panicking drivers and one particularly annoyed stallion. Sadly, as Dove rose with his own bows reloaded, one of the bolts caught him in the chest, toppling him back into the carriage roof in a spray of blood. Mia watched her Hand try to rise, lips painted blood, but the boy finally collapsed with a bubbling moan.*

"... I DID WARN YOU HE WAS AN IDIOT ..."

"... for once, we are in complete agreement ..."

Mia was on her feet, seeking cover amid the milling horses and panicked drivers. But with her arm cut to ribbons, there was no way she could steer a carriage and work the whip at the same time, and Aurelius's guards were closing fast.

Her gravebone dagger flashed, severing leather straps and couplings about a tall white stallion. Wincing at the pain, she dragged herself onto the stallion's back.

"... have you forgotten how much horses hate you ...?"

"Apparently so."

"... RIDE ...!"

Mia kicked the horse's flanks, the stallion bolted, hooves kicking up the packed gravel of the senator's yard as the guards roared at her to halt.* Crossbow bolts flew past her head, grazing her horse's flank, one bolt thudding into its hindquarters. The beast screamed, tried to throw her, but Mia clung on like a shadow to its owner's feet. The stallion put on a burst of speed, dashing past the front gate and out into the broad thoroughfares of the city of Galante. Bells tolled in the distance, echoing from dozens of different cathedrals, domes and minarets. The streets were crowded for Firemass, revelers shouting curses as Mia galloped past on her bleeding stallion.

The Blade glanced behind, saw half a dozen guards riding in pursuit. The blood pouring from her shoulder was sticky across her back, her sodden dress clinging to her skin. She was starting to feel light-headed from the loss. With a colorful curse, she snapped off the crossbow bolt in her backside, head swimming with agony. She needed to get off the streets, somewhere dark, hide until the noise died down.

Galante's streets were packed even here in the marrowborn district—too crowded to run a high-speed chase through much farther. Her stallion's burst of terrified speed was coming to an end, the horse now limping from the quarrel in its own hindparts. Mia slid off the hobbling beast, down into a crowd of drunken revelers, the cries of the pursuing guards ringing in her ears. She limped down an alley between one of the city's countless cathedrals and a looming administratii

---

*A note for would-be members of the law enforcement community: this *never* works.

building, twisting into the warren of the Galante backstreets. Gasping for breath, vision swimming, blood loss making her hands shake. Her left arm was entirely numb, Mister Kindly's voice in her ear urging her on. Finally, she found a wrought-iron fence, a crowded sea of headstones and tombs beyond it, run through with dark weeds and bright flowers.

Galante's necropolis.

She limped through the gate, stumbled down the tightly packed rows of marble and mossy granite, looming mausoleums, packed with generations of marrowborn dead. Finally, she ducked beneath the eave of a tomb belonging to some rich bastard, long ago forgotten. And reaching out to the shadows, Mia plucked them with clever fingers, weaving them about her shoulders.

As it always did, all the world fell to black beneath Mia's cloak. But she still heard Aurelius's guards as they entered the necropolis, boots tromping on the flagstones. Their captain barked an order and the group split up, weaving into the overcrowded labyrinth of crypts and vaults and tombs, cries of "Assassin!" ringing on the pale stone.

But one guard remained.

Mia could only dimly see him through her veil of shadows, but she could tell from his vague silhouette the man was huge. His boots crunched on the gravel as he slowly prowled the mausoleums, muttering softly. Mia held her breath as he walked closer to her hiding place, head moving side to side. She felt a warm trickle down her back, her flash of dread swallowed by her passengers as she realized that, despite her shadowcloak, her blood would have left a trail, and would now be pooling at her feet.

The guard prowled toward Mia's crypt. And rather than pray he'd pass her by, the girl simply threw aside her cloak and lunged, stiletto in hand.

The guard was wearing mail beneath his finery, but her gravebone blade pierced the steel rings as if they were butter. Her blow sank to the hilt, but striking blind, she'd landed shy of the fellow's heart. The big man cried aloud as she struck again, this time slicing his jugular. A spray of red hit her face, warm and wet, the guard seizing her wrist and delivering a crushing hook to her jaw. Mia was flung back against the tomb wall, lashing out at the hand that held her, the pair of them going down in a tumble.

His windpipe was still intact, and the guard was bellowing, the girl snarling, stabbing again and again. They rolled about on the flagstones, Eclipse and Mister Kindly both whispering warning that the other guards were returning. But her foe was huge, and for all her training, Mia was wounded, bleeding, and anyone who believes there's no advantage in being twice as big as your opponent has never fought a foe half their size.

She heard thundering boots, face twisted as the guard grabbed a fistful of her hair. Her blade finally found his neck again, sending him back onto the cobbles in a frothing red spray. Mia scrambled upright, saw another four guards approaching.

"...run...!"

"How?" she gasped.

"...HIDE...!"

"Where?"

"Halt!"

The guards fanned out around her, four clad in Senator Aurelius's finery. She could hear whistles in the distant street, the tromp tromp *of legionaries' boots. Fearless, even staring into the eyes of death, she glared at the tallest guard and twirled her stiletto through her fingers. She thought of Consul Scaeva and Cardinal Duomo. Her familia unavenged. But regret came ultimately from fear, and even there at the finish, she could find none inside her. Only rage that it could end like this.*

"Who dies first?" she asked, glaring at the assembled men.

The most sensible of the guards aimed a loaded crossbow at her chest.

"That'd be you, bitch," he spat.

A chill stole over her, dark and hollow. Goosebumps rippling on her bloodied skin. The suns burned high overhead, but here in the necropolis, the shadows were dark, almost black. A shape rose up behind the guards, hooded and cloaked, blades of what could only have been gravebone in its hands. It lashed out at the crossbow guard, hacked his head almost off his shoulders. The other guards cried out, raised their blades, but the figure moved like lightning, striking once, twice, three times. And almost faster than Mia could blink, all four guards were dead on the dirt.

"Maw's teeth," she whispered.

The shadows at her feet shivered, Eclipse coalescing with a growl. Mister Kindly was on her shoulder, puffed up and spitting. Mia felt the chill in her bones, her passengers swallowing her fear as her savior turned to face her.

Not human. That much was clear. O, it was shaped like a man beneath that cloak—tall and broad shouldered. But its hands...'byss and blood, the hands wrapped about its sword hilts were black. Tenebrous and semitranslucent, fingers coiled about the hilts like serpents. Mia couldn't see its face, but small, black tentacles writhed and wriggled from within the hollows of its hood, pulling the cowl lower over its features. And though it was near summersdeep, two suns burning high in the sky, its breath hung in white clouds before its lips, Mia's whole body shivering at the chill.

"...Who are you?"

"ASK THAT OF YOURSELF," the figure replied. Its voice was hollow, sibilant, tinged with a strange reverberation. "MIA CORVERE."

The girl blinked.

". . . You know me?"

The figure moved closer, in a way Mia could only describe as . . . slithering. A rime of frost creeping across the tombs and crypts around them.

"I KNOW THAT YOU ARE MEANT FOR MORE THAN THIS," it said. "YOUR TRUTH LIES BURIED IN THE GRAVE. AND YET YOU PAINT YOUR HANDS IN RED FOR THEM, WHEN YOU SHOULD BE PAINTING THE SKIES BLACK."

". . . o, joys, a cryptic one . . ."

"YOUR VENGEANCE IS AS THE SUNS, MIA CORVERE. IT SERVES ONLY TO BLIND YOU."

"What the fuck are you talking about?"

Mia heard shouts, turned toward the sound of approaching boots.

"SEEK THE CROWN OF THE MOON."

Turning back, she found the thing gone, as if it had never been. Her breath still hung white in the air, the chill receding slow from her bones, its voice ringing in the black behind her eyes. She looked about the graveyard, seeing only corpses and crypts and wondering if she were dreaming awake.

". . . mia, they are coming . . ."

". . . WE MUST GO . . ."

More whistles. Boots coming closer. Blood on her face and skin. Mia snatched up one of the guard's cloaks—the least bloody of the lot. And pulling the cowl over her head, she limped through the necropolis, quick as she could, struggling over the wrought-iron fence and disappearing into the warrens of the Galante backstreets.

Only bodies in her wake.

The Hanging Gardens of Ysiir are a sight unlike any under the suns.

In Godsgrave, the vast rooftop gardens of Little Liis overflow with sunsbride and honeyrose, helping to smother the sewer reek of the Rose River in their wondrous perfume. In Whitekeep, the garden mazes that King Francisco III built to entertain his mistresses stretch for miles, and an army of slaves toils to keep them trim, even a century after the monarchy's fall. The Thorn Towers of Elai stand seventy feet high, covered in vast tangles of razor-vine. When the vines bloom just before summersdeep, the towers are covered in blossoms than can be seen across the city. But no garden in all the Republic can match the Hanging Gardens of Ysiir, gentlefriends.

Not for their grandeur, nor their horror.

The smell struck Mia first. It rose over the stench in her cage miles from the city. Blood and sweat and blackest misery. She stared at the metropolis rising out of the haze ahead, chewing her lip. Some of the children in her wagon began to cry, younger women alongside them. Mia felt her shadow surge as she looked to their destination.

Never fear.

The Hanging Gardens had been settled by Liisian explorers after the Ysiiri Empire's fall. In the centuries since the collapse, the port had grown into the largest metropolis on the coast, and now served as the greatest hub in the south seas for the fuel that drove the Itreyan Republic's heart.

Slavery.

The cityport was red stone, nestled on the edge of a natural bay. The architecture was a blend of old Ysiiri ruins and graceful spires and domes of Liisian design built atop the old city's remains. And all around the city walls hung thousands of iron gibbets, filled with thousands of human bodies.

Some were decades old, only tattered bones inside. Some were fresh dead. But from the piteous wails rising over the bustling metropolis beyond, Mia knew hundreds still lived. Left to hang in their cages 'til they perished.

The Hanging Gardens of Ysiir. Its flowers made of flesh and bone.*

And Mia was here at last.

---

* The history of the Hanging Gardens is drenched in blood. Founded as a trade city, it quickly became a hub of flesh commerce after the rise of the Itreyan kings. But the port was originally named Ur-Dasis, meaning "Walled City" in the tongue of old Ysiir, and it was only after a revolt during the reign of Francisco II that the city received its new moniker.

With slave labor serving as the backbone of his kingdom, Francisco couldn't afford any sort of rebellion. When a group of slaves revolted against their captors and seized Ur-Dasis, the king sent an entire legion under the infamous general Atticus Dio to quash the revolt. Though the besieged rebels fought bravely, they were ultimately starved out, agreeing to surrender if Atticus promised mercy. The general agreed, vowing that the rebels would only be returned to captivity.

Predictably, Atticus didn't keep his word. When the rebels laid down their arms, they were strung up from the city walls in their thousands as a warning to any who'd dare revolt in future. Some of the original iron gibbets still decorate the city, and rebellious slaves meet the same fate even now—caged upon the walls to die in the blazing suns.

Francisco was so pleased with his general's performance, he renamed Ur-Dasis the Hanging Gardens in his honor.

Interestingly, Atticus himself was to lead a revolt against Francisco's grandson, the boy king Francisco IV, nearly twenty years later. And when said revolt failed, the gen-

The wagon train trundled through broad wooden gates, the stench rising with the heat. The streets were crowded, the harbor beyond filled with ships from all over the Republic, some off-loading, some shipping out laden with stock for resale. This was market season, when the slaver crews returned from their runs up the Ysiiri coast and farther east, their holds laden with fresh meat. Itreyan legionaries rubbed shoulders with Liisian merchants, and the din of coin and sorrow filled the air.

Mia felt someone push up beside her. Turning, she saw a thin woman staring out at the streets, her face pale.

"Everseeing help us . . ."

Mia squinted at the two suns above.

"I don't think he's listening," she murmured.

The wagon pulled to a halt at the market square's seething edge. Teardrinker hopped down from the driver's seat, limping to the rear of the women's wagon, pulling back the cover and pointing at Mia.

"All right, girl," she said. "Off to the Pit we go."

The captain unlocked the cage, stepped back with crossbow in hand. Merchants were already crowded around the wagon, prodding the stock inside and appraising their worth. Thugs in the market's employ began off-loading men from the rear wagon, shackles singing a rusted song as the captives hopped down on the hardpacked earth. Mia climbed out of the wagon, watching the crowd around them.

I'm here.

She hid her smile behind the matted locks of her hair.

One step closer.

The Pit was dug at the other end of the marketplace, and Mia could hear it well before she laid eyes on it. Ragged cheers and grunts of pain, the clink of coin and the crack of bone. As they made their way across the crowded square, Teardrinker was stopped at least a dozen times by merchants inquiring about Mia's sale. It took all the girl's will to keep her temper in check as she felt them pawing her curves, checking her teeth with dirty hands. But Teardrinker declined all offers for Mia's purchase, indicating she'd be for sale in the Pit soon. The captain's refusals were met with disbelief or dismay, one merchant declaring it a "waste of good tits." But Teardrinker held firm, and the pair walked on.

---

eral was transported to Ysiir and hung upon the same walls he had liberated two decades earlier.

History, gentlefriends, is not without a sense of irony.

The Pit was exactly that—a hole dug ten feet deep, fifty feet wide, hemmed with limestone walls. A broad stockyard was built beside it, rusted iron bars holding back a multitude of muscular slaves. It was encircled by limestone bleachers, packed with cheering gamblers and shouting bookmakers. And on the innermost ring, attended by the seconds and servants, she saw over a dozen sanguila.*

Mia stood with head bowed at the Pit's iron gates. Itreyan legionaries in plumed helmets were inspecting another slaver's stock before allowing him to pass. The girl whispered from beneath her tangled curtains of hair.

"Can you see Leonides?"

"Aye, there." Teardrinker nodded across the stockyard. "The fat bastard."

". . . They're *all* fat bastards."

"The fattest bastard, then."

Mia squinted, finally spying an Itreyan man seated under a broad parasol. He was dressed in a long frock coat despite the heat, his cravat knotted tight, pierced with a pin in the shape of a lion's head. His face was swarthy, his body pudgy from too many years of too much food and wine. Beside him sat another Itreyan, broad and muscular, watching the Pit with a keen eye.

"That's Titus," Teardrinker said. "He serves as executus, trains all of Leonides's stock."

"I know what an executus does," Mia muttered.

"Are you certain? Because if was a betting woman, I'd wager my last beggar you had *no* fucking idea what you're about."

"I told you," Mia replied. "Leonides has trained two of the last three champions of the *Venatus Magni*. He has qualifying berths in all the arenas. He bribes the right officials, owns the right people. If I'm to win my freedom, my best chance is training under him."

"But *why,* girl?" Teardrinker demanded. "You could've walked away free in the desert! 'Byss, I'll let you walk free *now*! You saved my hide from those raiders, and I pay my debts. Why in the Everseeing's name do you want to be gladiatii?"

"I made a promise," Mia said. "And I mean to keep it."

"What kind of promise could be kept in a place like this?"

---

*Literally, "blood masters." Keepers of human stables, who fight their stock in the various gladiatii arenas across the Republic.

Successful sanguila have popularity to rival the most beloved Itreyan senator, though they lack the noble blood that would allow them to stand for political office.

Most content themselves by crying themselves to sleep in the arms of beautiful concubines on vast piles of money.

"A red promise."

Teardrinker sighed and shook her head. "This is madness."

"*. . . she is wiser than she looks . . .*"

The whisper came from the shadow under Mia's matted hair, too soft for the captain to notice. Teardrinker pulled off her tricorn and dragged her hand over her scalp. She looked at Mia sidelong and sighed.

"A girl like you has no place in this sort of business."

"Believe me, Captain," Mia replied. "You've never met a girl like me."

Teardrinker cursed, but true to her word, the slaver made her way to the legionaries at the entrance. Both men nodded greetings, raised eyebrows at the scrawny slip shuffling along in chains beside her.

"You lost, Captain?" the big one asked.

"Pleasure pens are yonder," the bigger one nodded to the bay.

Teardrinker sniffed hard, spat into the dirt. "Step aside, you stinking whoresons. I've a trueborn fighter to hock and no time to jaw unless you're slinging coin."

The bigger one blinked at Mia. ". . . You plan on selling this slip to a sanguila?"

The legionaries burst into uproarious laughter, holding their sides like bad actors in a pantomime. Mia kept her head bowed as Teardrinker squared up to the first guard. Big as he was, the woman could look the man eye to eye.

"Have I ever sold chaff in here, Paulo?" She looked to the next man. "Don't tell me my business, you cocksure wanker. I know it well, and it's in the fucking Pit."

The soldiers looked at each other, a little abashed. And with small shrugs, the pair stepped aside and let Teardrinker and Mia out into the stockyard. A greasy man with a wax tablet took Teardrinker's name, a young boy with a crooked eye marked Mia's arm and the back of her tunic with a number in blue paint. She watched him while he worked, wondering where he came from, how he'd come to be here. Staring at the single arkemical circle tattooed on his cheek.*

---

* Slavery in the Itreyan Republic is a highly codified affair, with an army of administratii devoted to overseeing it. Slaves are broken into three main categories, and branded with an arkemical symbol on their cheek to indicate their standing.

   Slaves with one circle are the rank and file: chattel who serve as housebodies, laborers, brothel fodder, and the like. Two circles denote a person trained in military matters: gladiatii, houseguards, and members of the Itreyan slave legion—the infamous Bloody Thirteenth. Folk marked with three circles are the rarest and most valuable, their

Taking Mia by the shackles, the boy started dragging her toward the other slaves. The girl resisted for a moment, looked Teardrinker in the eye.

"One more thing, Captain," she said softly.

"O, aye?" The captain raised an eyebrow. "Owed so many favors, are you?"

"You owe me your life. I'd call that the Largest Kind of Favor There Is. One turn, I might call in that marker. And it'd be lovely if I didn't have to ask you twice."

Teardrinker breathed deep. "As I said, girl, I pay my debts."

Satisfied, Mia let herself be dragged away, standing in the sweltering heat with the other human livestock. Looking around, she realized she was one of only two females, and the other woman was a Dweymeri with hands the size of dinner plates. She kept her eyes straight ahead, watching proceedings out in the Pit and avoiding the curious stares of her pen-mates.

It seemed a simple enough process. Fleshmongers like Teardrinker wandered the bleachers, spruiking their wares to the sanguila. And one at a time, their offerings were handed a wooden sword, and thrown face-first into a fight for their lives.

There were half a dozen professional fighters at work in the Pit's center, each a mountain of muscle and scars. When a new prospect was pushed into the ring, a random fighter would promptly heft a wooden sword and set about trying to bash their head in. Bets would be placed, the crowd would bay and howl, and if the competitor was still standing after a few minutes, the sanguila were given the opportunity to bid for their purchase. Those who fought with promise were snatched up. Those who failed were dragged away for resale somewhere else in the Hanging Garden.

Mia glanced at Sanguila Leonides. The man was considering matches the way spiders consider flies, but he never made a bid. The Lions of Leonides were the finest gladiatii in the Republic, and Leonides spent six months a year trawling coastal markets, handpicking the finest. If Mia wanted to call him Domini, she'd need to impress.

Fortunately, one didn't become a Blade of the Red Church by being a slouch with a sword.

The ledgerman called Mia's number. The holding pen door opened. The crook-eyed boy unlocked her shackles, handed her a dented wooden gladius

---

brand indicating they're possessed of an education or some exceptional skill: scribes, musicians, majordomo, and some highly prized courtesans.

And if you're wondering why skilled prostitutes are so valued in the Republic, gentlefriends, you've obviously never spent the night with a skilled prostitute.

that she wouldn't have used for firewood under normal circumstances. And without ceremony, Mia found herself shoved into the middle of the Pit.

Jeers rang across the stands, choking guffaws and fountains of abuse. The sight of the skinny, black-haired girl standing knock-kneed in the center of the ring didn't seem to be impressing the plebs in the crowd, let alone the blood masters.

"Aa's burning cock, is this a joke?" one yelled.

Spit and curses rained into the Pit, the various sanguila turning disinterested eyes to their ledgers—whatever this jest was, it was clear not a one of them found it amusing. One of the pit fighters raised an eyebrow at the ledgerman, who simply nodded. The man shrugged and hefted his wooden sword, striding toward Mia. He was a Dweymeri, broad as bridges, brown skin glistening with sweat.

"Hold still, lass," he growled. "This won't hurt long."

Mia did as she was bid, standing motionless as the big man closed. But as the giant raised his blade to stove her skull in, the girl moved. Quick as shadows.

A sidestep, the blade whistling past her head. Mia cracked her wooden gladius down on the man's wrist, shattering bone. Several sanguila turned to stare as the big man screamed. Mia kicked savagely at his knee, rewarded with a nauseating crunch as the joint bent entirely the wrong way. The big man dropped with a bellow, and with deliberate brutality, Mia slammed her wooden blade directly into his throat, smashing his larynx to sauce.

Red froth spattered the man's lips as he turned astonished eyes to Mia. The girl slung her hair over her shoulder, whispering soft.

"*Hear me, Niah,*" she whispered. "*Hear me, Mother. This flesh your feast. This blood your wine. This life, this end, my gift to you. Hold him close.*"

And with a gurgle, the pit fighter toppled dead into the dirt.

Bewildered murmurs rippled among the crowd. Mia curtseyed to the sanguila, like a new dona at her debut ball. Then she turned to the next fighter in the row and leveled her wooden sword at his head.

"You're next, prettyboy."

The fighter (who *was* rather pretty) looked to his fellows, the corpse on the ground, and finally to the ledgerman. The greasy fellow glanced up at the sanguila, who were now staring at Mia intently. And turning back to the swordsman, he nodded.

The fighter stepped forward, Mia skipped up to meet him. Their match lasted less than ten seconds, ending with Mia's bootprint embedded in the man's crotch and her wooden sword shoved down his pretty throat, all the way to the hilt. The girl turned to the crowd and curtseyed again.

"A hundred priests," came the call.

"One hundred and ten."

Mia smiled behind her hair as sanguila began bidding. Within moments, her bid was two hundred silver coins—a decent sum by anyone's measure. But as she looked up into the bleachers, she saw Leonides and Titus hadn't uttered a word. Though the sanguila watched her intently, though Teardrinker was whispering in Titus's ear and he was nodding slow, Leonides didn't raise his voice to bid.

Time to stoke the flame.

Mia retrieved her wooden blade from the dead fighter's throat, turned to the third and spoke loud enough for the bleachers to hear.

"You. Next."

The big man looked at the two corpses at Mia's feet.

"Fuck that," he scoffed.

"Bring your friends." Mia smiled at the fighters beside him. "I've always wanted to try three at once."

The girl tossed her wooden sword onto the dirt.

"Or are you cowards all?"

The crowd hooted and jeered, and the fighters rankled. To be bested on their own soil was one thing, but to eat a plateful of shit from an unarmed girl half their size was another. With flashing eyes and swords raised, the men stepped out into the Pit.

With a dark smile, the girl stepped up to meet them.

CHAPTER 4

OFFERING

"Maw's teeth, are we going to be here 'til truelight?" Mia snarled.

Pietro raised an eyebrow, poured another measure of goldwine onto her bloody shoulder. Mia winced in pain, took a drag of her cigarillo with a shaking hand. She was sat on a low stone bench, Pietro behind her, swathed in his customary black robes. The Hand was busy sewing up the bloody gouge in her shoulder, and he'd padded a wad of gauze about her backside, soaking through with red.

The chamber was sparse, dark stone walls and dim arkemical globes. Like most rooms in the Galante Chapel, it was perfumed with the faint stench of shit. The servants of Our Lady of Blessed Murder here in the Cityport of Churches* had built their hideaway among the vast network of sewers beneath Galante's skin, and it was hard to escape the smell. In the eight months she'd served here, Mia had become accustomed to it, but as a preference spent as little time down here as possible. Unless she needed stitching up or resupply, she really only visited when she needed to speak to—

"Well, bugger me all the way backwards," said a familiar voice. "Look what the shadowcat dragged in."

Mia looked up, saw a woman standing in the doorway, dressed in leather britches, long boots, and a black velvet shirt. She was finger-thin, light brown hair cut in a distinctly masculine style, dark shadows under her eyes. She walked with a singular swagger, and wore more knives than anyone in her right mind would know what to do with.

"Bishop Tenhands," Mia said, inclining her head. "I'd stand and bow, but the crossbow bolt in my backside isn't too agreeable."

"An interesting nevernight, then," the woman smirked.

"Some coul—ow, fuck!" Mia glared over her shoulder again. "'Byss and blood, Pietro, are you stitching me up or sewing a dress?"

---

* Galante proudly boasts the greatest number of churches and temples in all the Republic, besting even Godsgrave in the tally.

Before the great Unifier, King Francisco I, conquered the nation, the people of Liis worshiped a holy trinity known as the Father, the Mother, and the Child. But once assimilated by the Itreyan monarchy, worship of the God of Light caught on among the common folk like a fire in a well-stocked brewery.

One wily fellow, a merchant named Carlino Grimaldi, decided the best way to distinguish himself in the new world order was to chuck wagonloads of money at the Itreyan church. He built the first cathedral to Aa in all of Liis; a towering structure known as Basilica Lumina, right in the heart of Galante. Sculpted of rare purple marble and beautiful stained glass, construction almost bankrupted its patron. However, so impressive was the final result, Galante's cardinal had Grimaldi appointed as governor of the entire city. Galante nobles were soon falling over themselves to curry favor among Aa's ministry, and churches to the Everseeing and temples to his four daughters began springing up over Galante like a rash on a sugargirl's nethers after the navy hits town.

Though he was later crucified for tax evasion, Carlino still went down in Liisian history as an Exceptionally Clever Bastard. Even to this turn, to curry favor among men of the cloth in Liis is known as "pulling a Grimaldi."

"All right, all right, bugger off," Tenhands told the beleaguered surgeon. "I'll finish her up. I'd like a word with our Blade alone."

"My Bishop," Pietro nodded, slapping a bundle of gauze none too gently on Mia's bleeding shoulder and leaving the room. Tenhands sauntered around behind Mia, pulled away the bandage, the girl wincing as the blood stuck it to her skin.

Tenhands was a figure of infamy in Red Church lore, a long-serving Blade of the Mother with near twenty sanctified kills to her name. Old Mercurio had told Mia tales about the woman when she was younger, and Mia had grown up as something of an admirer.* Serving in the Cityport of Churches, she'd learned its bishop wasn't much for civility. Or frivolity. But she liked results, so fortunately, Tenhands liked her.

"This looks like it hurts," Tenhands muttered, eyeing the horrid wound across Mia's back and shoulder.

"It's far from ticklish."

The bishop took up the bone needle, began sewing Mia's wound with steady fingers. "I trust the pain was worth it?"

Mia winced, taking a long drag of her clove cigarillo. "Senator Aurelius's son is being fitted for his death masque as we speak."

"You used the lament?"

Mia nodded. "On the lips, just as you suggested."

"I shan't ask how you got access to the young don's mouth, then."

"Never kiss and tell."

"And where's young Dove?"

"Sadly," Mia sighed, "my young Hand won't be back for supper. Ever."

"Shame, that."

---

* Tenhands began her career as a thief on the streets of Elai, and even after she became a Blade of the Mother, she never lost her knack for the art of stealth. She was said to move like the dark itself, and was capable of dislocating both shoulders at will, allowing her to squeeze through the tightest of places with little difficulty.

Her most infamous Offering was a senator named Phocas Merinius—a man so astonishingly paranoid about assassination, it was said he kept a retinue of half a dozen guards on hand at his bedside when he made love to his wife. Tenhands reportedly gained access to Phocas's villa by crawling in through the sewer and up the privy spout—an ingress eight inches wide at best—and lying in wait right there inside the pipe. When poor Phocas heard the call of nature in the middle of the nevernight, he sat down on the privy seat and found both his femoral arteries severed before he could even commence his business.

Tenhands reportedly spent the next seven turns in the chapel's baths trying to wash off the stink.

The things we do for our Mothers . . .

"He was never the sharpest blade on the racks, Bishop."

"Beggars can't be choosers." Tenhands dug the needle in for another stitch. *"Since the Järnheims gutted us, quality around here is in short supply. Present company excepted, of course."*

Mia chewed her lip and sighed. Bishop Tenhands spoke truth—good Hands and Blades were hard to find in the Red Church these turns. Galante was never a glamorous appointment, and most of the servants of Niah posted here dreamed of grander things. But matters were worse than ever since the Luminatii attack.

Eight months on, Our Lady of Blessed Murder's congregation was still bleeding from the blow Ashlinn Järnheim and her brother had inflicted at the behest of their father. It wasn't simply Lord Cassius's murder that had the Church reeling, although the loss of the Black Prince would have been grievous enough. But Torvar Järnheim hadn't merely had his children serve up the Ministry to the Luminatii—the old assassin had also revealed the location of every Red Church chapel in the Republic.

And so, while Justicus Remus was invading the Quiet Mountain, the Luminatii had launched simultaneous assaults across greater Itreya. The chapels in Dweym and Galante remained unscathed.* But every other chapel had been destroyed.

Worse, Torvar had supplied names. Aliases. Last known residences. Between Torvar's treachery and the Luminatii attacks, Our Lady of Blessed Murder had lost near three-quarters of her assassins in a single nevernight.

As the bishop said, the Red Church had been gutted; that was probably the only reason a Blade as young as Mia was even entrusted with offerings like the one on Gaius Aurelius. In the eight months since her posting to Galante, she'd ended

---

*The Luminatii raids had missed both: the Galante Chapel was only recently constructed, and unbeknownst to the Järnheims, the old Dweym Chapel had been relocated the previous winter, when, due to unusually heavy rains and some dodgy plumbing, its cellar (and thus, its blood pool) had flooded.

Instead of refilling the pool, the Ministry decided to build a new structure on higher ground in the cityport of Seawall, and abandoned the ruined one in Farrow. If constructing an entirely new chapel to Our Lady of Blessed Murder, in secret, in the middle of a major metropolis, seems a costly and cumbersome affair, consider the following:

1. Two thousand–odd cubic feet of *vitus* fills every Church blood pool.
2. There are approximately seven and a half gallons of liquid per cubic foot.
3. The average pig holds approximately one gallon of blood in its body.

Do the math, gentlefriends. And ask yourself if you ever want to be filling one of these damn pools twice.

three men and one woman in the Black Mother's name. Most Blades her age would be lucky to have been sent on their first kill.

Mia was thankful for the chance to show her worth. But problem was, her list of throats to slit was growing longer, not shorter. She'd killed Justicus Remus, but Consul Scaeva and Grand Cardinal Duomo still lived. Her familia were still unavenged. And with Tric's murder at Ashlinn's hands during the Luminatii attack, she now had one more windpipe to open before her vengeance was done.

And stuck here in Galante, she was no closer to any of them.

Mia clenched her jaw as the bishop continued to stitch her, thinking about . . . that . . . thing that had accosted her in the necropolis. Truth was, it had saved her life. Her near-death should have left her shaken, but as ever, her passengers ate any sense of fear inside her, twice as swift now as when she carried Mister Kindly alone. She felt nothing close to afraid. And so, she was only left with questions.

What was it?

What did it want with her?

"The Crown of the Moon"?

She'd seen that particular phrase before, buried in the pages of—

"Heard about some trouble with Aurelius's guards," Tenhands remarked, ceasing her needlework long enough to take a pull of the medicinal goldwine.

"Nothing I couldn't handle," Mia replied.

"You normally operate with a little more discretion."

"Beg pardon, Bishop, but you didn't ask for discretion," Mia said, faint annoyance in her voice. "You asked for a dead senator's son."

"One doesn't necessarily preclude the other."

"But given the choice, which would you rather?"

Mia hissed as the bishop poured more alcohol onto her now-closed wound, bound it in long strips of gauze.

"I like you, Corvere," Tenhands said. "You remind me of me in my younger turns. More balls than most men I've ever met. And you get your killing done, so you've earned a little ego. But word to the wise: you'd best leave that lip of yours behind when you head back to the Mountain. The Ministry aren't as fond of you as I."

"And why would I head back to the Mountain? I'm posted to—"

"Speaker Marius sent a blood missive just now," Tenhands interjected. "You've been recalled by the Ministry."

Mia's eyes narrowed in suspicion. Goosebumps on her skin.

". . . Why?" she asked.

Tenhands shrugged. "All I know is they're leaving me a killer down, and a pile *of throats that need slitting. If I could use Blades on more than one offering at a time, that'd be something. But that'd breach the Promise.* So when you see that bastard Solis, be a love and knee him in the codpiece for me, will you?"*

---

* It is commonly known among folk who employ hired killers that the Red Church operates under a code of, if not outright *honor,* then at least *conduct,* known as the Red Promise. The strictures are thus:

- Inevitability—no offering undertaken in the history of the Church has *ever* gone unfulfilled.
- Sanctity—a current employer of the Church may not be chosen as a target of the Church.
- Secrecy—the Church does not discuss the identity of its employers.
- Fidelity—a Blade will only serve one employer a time.
- Hierarchy—all offerings must be approved by the Lord/Lady of Blades or Revered Father/Mother.

The first three strictures were loosely in place at the Church's inception, but the strictures of Fidelity and Hierarchy were codified after an infamous event in Church history, told to acolytes as "The Tale of Flavius and Dalia."

Take a pew, gentlefriends.

Flavius Apullo was an Itreyan general who stood among the conspirators who overthrew King Francisco XV and forged the Republic. He went on to become a senator, and as one does, immensely wealthy.

The period around the collapse of the Itreyan monarchy was a busy time in the art of professional murder, and authority was being granted to individual bishops of local chapels to accept offerings. Senator Flavius Apullo began fearing assassination around the same time his rivals got serious about bumping him off, and in an embarrassing turn, the Red Church undertook to murder Flavius the very same nevernight as he employed a Church Blade on retainer as his bodyguard.

Red faces all around, gentlefriends.

In a further cluster of fuckery, the Blade designated for *both* these offerings was a woman named Dalia. Beautiful, manipulative, and peerless with a punching dagger, Dalia served as Flavius's bodyguard for three years. In that time, the pair became lovers, and Dalia eliminated a slew of Flavius's rivals—all save his most vocal opponent, Tiberius the Elder. Tiberius was the senator who'd employed the Church to murder Flavius, and under the Law of Sanctity, he was off-limits until said murder was complete. Tiberius, however, was dying of Old Mother Syphilis, and in quite a hurry to see Flavius necked before he shuffled off this mortal coil.

The Red Church was on the brink of a political embarrassment that could have ended their reputation.

Cleverly, Flavius proposed marriage to Dalia to cement her place at his side—he assumed a fiancée would keep him safer from any would-be assassins than a mere employee. Not so cleverly, he let his patronage with the Red Church lapse the same turn that Dalia accepted his marriage proposal.

Dalia stabbed her husband to death on their wedding night. Rumor conflicts whether she wept as she did the deed. She brought Flavius's head to the sickbed of

Mia's mind was turning, suspicion and excitement entwined in her belly. Being recalled by the Ministry could mean anything. Reassignment. Rebuke. Retribution. She'd served the Black Mother well in the past eight months, but every Shahiid in the Mountain knew she'd failed her final trial, refusing to kill an innocent. The only reason she became a Blade at all was because Lord Cassius had baptized her as he lay dying on the sands of Last Hope. Perhaps the good grace his endorsement had given her had finally run out . . .

Who knew what awaited her when she arrived?

"When do I leave?" Mia asked.

Tenhands lifted her bone needle, looked meaningfully at Mia's backside.

"As soon as you can walk."

Mia sighed. No sense fretting on what she couldn't change. And getting back to the Mountain, she could speak to Chronicler Aelius again, see Naev. Maybe find some of the answers she sought.

"Bend over," the bishop ordered. "I'll try to be gentle."

Mia took the bottle of medicinal goldwine and took a long, deep pull.

"I'll bet you say that to all the girls."

I t turns out three men at once was almost more than Mia could handle.

The battle had started well enough. The pit fighters had advanced, spurred on by the jeering crowd and the fact that Mia had thrown her wooden sword into the dirt. The first—a burly Itreyan—had bellowed a war cry and swung his blade at her head. And with a glance, Mia had reached toward the dark at his feet.

Out here in the light of two suns, the shadows were sluggish and heavy. But Mia was stronger now, in herself, in what she was, and she'd been playing this particular trick for years, after all. With a glance, she affixed the big Itreyan's boots in his own shadow, stopping his charge short. Weaving close as he lost balance, she'd kicked him hard in the knee, punched him square in the throat, and as he toppled backward, she'd pirouetted and caught the sword flying from his hand to the tune of the cheering crowd.

Tiberius the Elder to prove the contract was fulfilled. And content the Church's reputation was intact, but more, that Tiberius was no longer a Church employer protected by the Law of Sanctity, Livia raised her punching dagger and saved Old Mother Syphilis the trouble.

Rumors about whether she was weeping at the time are quite clear.

After this incident, it was decided to write some actual bloody rules about how things would be run around here.

"*. . . you are showing off now . . . ,*" came a whisper in her ear.

"That's the bloody poin—"

The blow caught her on the back of the head, sent her reeling. She barely managed to turn and block the next flurry, staggering back into a semblance of guard. The remaining pit fighters—a broad Liisian with a pockmarked face, and a taller Dweymeri with only seven fingers—advanced, giving her no time to catch her breath. She was forced back across the Pit, warm blood dripping down the back of her neck.

Sevenfingers stepped up, swung at her face, throat, chest. Mia countered, locking him up and slipping inside his guard, but Pockface's sword cracked across her ribs before she could strike, and an elbow sent her sprawling into the dirt.

She kept her grip on her sword, rolling aside as the pair tried to stomp her head in. Scrabbling on the ground, she slung a handful of red sand into Pockface's eyes, lashed out with her boot and sent Sevenfingers to the ground. Rolling to her feet, she planted her boot in the now-blinded Pockface's bollocks, hard enough to elicit a groan of sympathy from every man in the crowd. And to their cheers, she smashed her sword hilt into his face, smearing his nose across his cheeks.

"*. . . behind . . .*"

She turned, barely blocking a blow that would've caved her skull in. The burly Itreyan was back on his feet, chin smeared with vomit and spit. She danced with him in the dust, strike and riposte, weave and flurry. Burlyboy was huge, twice as strong as she. But what Mia lacked in size, she made up for in speed and sheer, bloody ferocity. The Itreyan swung hard, snapping her gladius in half as she blocked. But with a shapeless cry, she danced inside his follow-through, crouched low and smashed her broken sword up beneath his chin. The splintered wood punctured his throat, gouts of blood coating Mia's hands as Burlyboy fell.

"*. . . left, left . . . !*"

Mister Kindly's whisper brought her around, but too late—a gladius caught her across the shoulder, sent her reeling as the crowd roared. Sevenfingers swung again, struck her in the ribs, Mia gasping in agony. She locked up his sword-arm, pulled him close. Smelling sweat, dirty breath, blood. Sevenfingers punched her in the face, once, twice, and with a ragged cry she reached out to the shadows, locking up his feet as she pushed backward with all her strength. With his feet rooted, the man toppled backward, Mia falling on top of him, fingers finding his mouth, slipping inside his cheeks and twisting like fishhooks before ripping outward.

The man screamed as his lips split, the crowd baying. The girl began pounding on his jaw with her fists, once, twice, three times. Hands red. Teeth gritted. Blood in her mouth. Picturing a smiling consul with dark, pretty eyes. A grand cardinal with a beard like a hedgerow and a voice like honey. Their faces pulped as she pounded, again

"... *mia* ..."

and again, picturing her mother, her brother, her father, everything she'd lost, everything they'd *taken,* and this man beneath her just one more enemy, just one more obstacle between her and the turn she'd spit on all their fucking grav—

"... *mia* ...!"

She fell still. Drenched in sweat. Breath burning. Covered in warm, sticky red. She could feel Mister Kindly's chill, mixed with the blood on the back of her neck. The world came back into focus, its volume swelling in her ears. And beneath the thundering pulse and echoes of her past, she heard it. Swelling in her chest and tingling her fingertips.

Applause.

She stood, painted to the elbows in red. The crowd in the bleachers were on their feet, Teardrinker tending a flurry of bids rolling in from the sanguila at the Pit's edge. *Three hundred silver. Three hundred fifty. Four.* And on trembling legs, the girl walked across the Pit and stood before Leonides. She looked her would-be master in the eye, and dropped into a perfect curtsey before him.

"Domini," she said.

The sanguila regarded her with narrowed eyes. His executus whispered in his ear. And as a storm of butterflies took wing in Mia's belly, Leonides raised his hand and spoke in a voice that rang across the entire Pit.

"One thousand silver pieces."

A low murmur rippled across the audience, Mia's heart thrilling. Such a sum! Truth told, it was an overbid—the man could have probably knocked out most of his fellows with half that. But Mia knew the domini of the Lions of Leonides was fond of theater, and his bid told everyone in the Pit that he was in no mood to haggle.

Leonides wanted her. And so, he would have her. Price be damned.

It had gone perfectly. If Mia fought among the Lions of Leonides, she was almost assured a place in the *Venatus Magni.* And when the games were over, when she stood victorious upon the dais—

"One thousand and one," came a call.

Mia's belly turned cold. She glanced up to the stands, saw a figure step forward from the crowd. Wrapped in a long cloak despite the heat, pulling back the hood to reveal a young pretty face, long auburn hair, pale Itreyan skin.

A woman.

"*. . . who is that . . . ?*"

"No bloody idea," Mia whispered.

"One thousand and one silver pieces," the woman repeated.

Mia's eyes narrowed. She'd never heard of a female sanguila—though there had been a few famous female gladiatii, the stage of the *venatus* was ever managed by the careful hands of men. Maybe the newcomer was an agent for another domini? A foil from the ledgermen to drive up her price?

Mia looked to Leonides expectantly. Whoever this woman was, the greatest sanguila in the history of the games wasn't going to be outbid by a single silver coin.

Titus's face was a mask. Leonides glanced to his executus, back to the newcomer, speaking as if the words soured his mouth.

"This is somewhat childish, don't you think, my dear?"

The woman's smile was splashed across her face like poison.

"Childish? Whatever do you mean?"

"I hear tell you have but a handful of coppers to rub together," Leonides said. "If your intent is to embarrass the *patriis familia* of your own House, are there not less expensive ways to do so?"

The woman smiled wider, and Mia's stomach sank.

"My thanks for your concern," she said. "But this is just business, Father."

"*. . . o, dear . . .*"

"I have told you before, Leona," Leonides warned. "The *venatus* is no place for women. And the sanguila's box is no place for you."

"Frightened my Falcons might eclipse your Lions, dear Patriis?"

Leonides scoffed. "One victor's laurel in a backwater stoush does not a collegium make."

"You won't mind if I take the bloody beauty, then?"

Leona glanced at Mia. Leonides also turned to stare. Mia stepped forward, pleas roiling behind her teeth. But Mister Kindly's whisper held her still.

"*. . . remember who you are. and who you are supposed to be . . .*"

The not-cat was right. This was *her* script, after all, and she had the hardest role to play. If she was to fight on the sands in service to a gladiatii collegium, she could only do so as its property. And property didn't speak unless spoken to. It certainly didn't wade into a public pissing contest between father and daughter . . .

Shit.

Mia stared at Sanguila Leonides. Eyes pleading. She'd calculated it so well. She'd fought like a daemon, won the approval of every blood master in the Pit. She was only a single word, a *single bid* away from entry into the greatest collegium in the Republic. One step closer to Consul Scaeva's and Cardinal Duomo's throats. All Leonides need do was speak . . .

"Very well, Leona."

Leonides feigned a shrug, turning his back on his daughter.

"Take her, then. For all the good she will do you."

Leona smiled, sharp and bright. Mia's shoulders sagged. Legionaries marched into the ring, the crook-eyed boy slapping shackles around her wrists. She could've run then. Hidden beneath her cloak of shadows, slipped from the Pit with only dismayed shouts and prayers to the Everseeing in her wake.

But then she'd be right back where she started. It had taken weeks to orchestrate a clandestine trip to Ysiir, the broken caravan, her sale in the Garden. She'd waste weeks more in trying to get sold to a mightier collegium, and with the grand games so close, they were weeks she simply didn't have to spare.

She'd ended too many lives, risked so much to be here to simply abandon her plan altogether. And though Leona was an unknown factor, Mia still had faith in her own abilities, and no real fear she could fail. Behind her lay only blood and a Mountain full of treachery. Ahead lay the sand of the *venatus,* and vengeance.

This was her course now. For good or ill, she had to walk it.

The legionaries parted. Mia looked up to see Dona Leona standing before her. This close, she could see the woman was in her early twenties. Bright blue eyes and auburn hair coiled in gentle ringlets, lightly freckled skin. She wore gold jewelry, a ruby wedding band. Beneath her cloak, her gown was cut of soft Liisian silk. Every part of her screamed "wealth," save her eyes. As Mia risked a glance into those kohled pools of brilliant blue, she could think of only one word to describe them.

Hungry.

"My bloody beauty," she smiled. "What a pair we shall make."

Mia hung still, unsure what to say. Leona glanced at the soldiers, annoyance in her gaze. One of the men drew a truncheon, struck Mia across her legs. The girl cried out, fell to her knees. Teeth clenched, bloodstained hands in fists. But she could feel Mister Kindly, prowling cool inside her shadow, his whisper in her ears.

"*. . . who you are, and who you are supposed to be . . .*"

And so, she stayed there in the dust, eyes downturned, silent and still.

"I am Dona Leona," the woman said. "Though you will call me Domina."

The woman extended her hand. Mia saw a golden ring on Leona's signet finger—a falcon, wings spread, crowned with a victor's wreath.

The truncheon cracked across her shoulder blades. Mia gasped in pain.

"Show your respects, slave!" a soldier barked.

Mia stared at that bird of prey in its wreath of gold. Just as proud and fierce and wild as she. And yet here she was, kneeling in the dirt like a whipped kitten.

Patience, she thought.

If Vengeance has a mother, her name is Patience.

Mia drew a deep breath.

Closed her eyes.

"Domina," she murmured.

And leaning forward, she kissed the ring.

CHAPTER 5

DEVOTION

Pig's blood has a very peculiar taste.

The blood of a man is best drunk warm, and leaves a hint of sodium and rust clinging to the teeth. Horse's blood is less salty, with an odd bitterness almost like dark chocolate. But pig's blood has an almost buttery quality, like oysters and oiled iron, slipping down your throat and leaving a greasy tang in its wake.

Mia fucking hated it, truth told.

She burst from the pool of red with a gasp, a thudding pulse still ringing in her ears, head spinning. She was naked save for a gravebone stiletto at her wrist, a gravebone sword at her waist, long black hair glued like ropes of weed to bloody skin. A rectangular package wrapped in oilskin was clutched in her fingers. Two Hands in dark robes stood in the pool beside her, helping her to her feet as she gasped and sputtered and pawed the gore from her lashes.

Blinking around the room, she found herself waist-deep in a triangular marble pool of blood, thirty feet at a side—Speaker Marius's chambers within the Quiet

Mountain. The room was carved with sorcerii glyphs, the heavy scent of butchery in the air. Maps of every city in the Republic were painted on the wall in blood.

Mia licked her teeth and spat, dragged her hair from her eyes.

Looking to the head of the pool, Mia saw Blood Speaker Marius, knelt on the stone. Though she'd not admit it to any, her belly thrilled a little at the sight of him. Weaver Marielle could make a portrait of any face, but her brother was her masterpiece—high cheekbones and a chiseled jaw. His skin was ghostly pale, his tousled hair snow white. He wore a red silk robe, open at the chest, the troughs and valleys of his chest carved in marble. His leather britches rode so low on his hips they were almost indecent, and the V-shaped cut of his abdom—

"Good turn to thee, Blade Mia," the sorcerer said.

Mia dragged her stare back up to eyes the color of blood.

"And you, Speaker."

Marius's pretty lips twisted in a knowing smile, but Mia kept her face like stone. The speaker was a picture, no doubt. And Mia had entertained her share of fantasies; lying in bed and picturing his pale, clever fingers as her own roamed ever lower. She'd even saved his and his beloved sister's lives during the Luminatii attack. But Mia couldn't fool herself into thinking of him as anything but a black-hearted bastard.

Still. A fuckable bastard . . .

"The Ministry await thee in the Hall of Eulogies," Marius said.

Mia waded out of the pool, still limping from her wounds, careful of slipping on the bloody tile. She was conscious of the speaker's stare on her naked body, the blood sloshing like a gentle sea. Mia looked down the hall to the stairwell leading up to the waiting Ministry. Wondering why the 'byss she'd been called here.

With a final glance to the speaker, Mia walked from the room. Washing off the drying blood and changing silently; black leathers and wolfskin boots, a shirt of dark linen. She hid her gravebone stiletto in her sleeve, hung her beautiful gravebone longsword from the scabbard at her waist. The former had belonged to her mother, the latter to her father, taken from the dead hand of Justicus Remus. Both blades had hilts fashioned like crows in flight, eyes of red amber. They were all she had left of her parents, aside her name.

She supposed there was a metaphor in there somewhere . . .

Unwrapping her oilskin package, she took the beaten leatherbound book inside under her arm and trudged up the stairs.* The voice of a ghostly choir hung

---

* Mia often counted stairs in the Mountain as she climbed them. She was never surprised when the tally changed. Some of the more "temperamental" flights, such as the one leading to the Hall of Song, shifted constantly, whereas the flight leading to

in the black, and Mia couldn't help but smile at the familiar song. After months in Galante, she'd returned to the hallowed halls of the most feared assassins in all the Itreyan Republic.

At last, she'd come home.

After an interminable climb, she stepped out into the Hall of Eulogies. The space was vast, circular, carved into the Quiet Mountain's granite heart. A beautiful statue of Niah, Mother of Night and Our Lady of Blessed Murder, loomed forty feet above Mia's head. A set of scales hung in her right hand, a wickedly sharp sword in her left. Wherever Mia stood in the room, Niah's eyes seemed to follow.

The space was ringed with pillars thicker than ancient ironwoods. The walls were lined with tombs, scarlet light washing through huge stained-glass windows. On the flagstones, Mia could see the names of every one of the Red Church's victims— thousands of lives claimed in their Black Mother's name. In contrast, the tombs were unmarked. They contained bodies of servants of the Mother and in death, only the Mother mourned them.

Mia's eyes drifted to a tomb in the western wall. The four small letters she'd scratched into the stone with a gravebone blade eight months ago.

"Blade Mia," said a deep voice. "Welcome home."

Mia turned to the foot of the statue. The entire Red Church Ministry was assembled, watching with expectant gazes.

All except Revered Father Solis, of course.

The big Itreyan stood with blind eyes turned to the soaring gables. He was clad in a robe of fine gray cloth, his hood pulled back. Pale blond stubble dusted a scarred scalp, his beard set in four resin spikes. His ever-empty scabbard hung at his side, the leather embossed with concentric circles.

To Solis's right stood Spiderkiller, Shahiid of Truths. The elegant Dweymeri was clad in emerald green, gold at her throat. Her saltlocks were artfully coiled atop her head. Hands and lips stained black from poisoncraft.

To Solis's left stood Mouser, Shahiid of Pockets, his handsome face belying the years in his twinkling eyes. An Ysiiri blacksteel blade hung as his side, two naked figures with feline heads entwined on the hilt. He was rolling a coin across the knuckles of his right hand, his left clutching an ornate cane—his legs had been badly broken during the Luminatii invasion, and the Shahiid would limp for the rest of his life.

---

the Sky Altar seemed almost lazy by comparison. Interestingly enough, the stairs leading up to the chambers of the Hall of Eulogies remained constant in number.

Three hundred thirty-three.

Third was Aalea, Shahiid of Masks. Milk-white skin and blood-red lips, curtains of black hair framing a face that made the word "beauty" hang its head in shame. She smiled at Mia as if the whole world were a secret and only she knew the answer. Promising to share it as soon as the pair were alone.

To date, there had been no new Shahiid of Song appointed—Solis was still teaching fresh acolytes the art of steel until a suitable replacement could be found. Wounds from the Järnheims' assault were fresh, and even here, in the seat of the Church's power in the Republic, the scabs remained.

"Shahiids," Mia said, bowing low. "I return, as requested."

"As commanded," Solis growled.

". . . Forgiveness, Revered Father. Commanded."

The title tasted strange on Mia's tongue. After Cassius's death, it was fitting that Revered Mother Drusilla become the Lady of Blades, but Drusilla's decision to appoint Solis as Revered One had vexed Mia more than a little. Solis still bore the tiny scar on his face from where Mia had bested him in the Hall of Song, and her arm still sometimes tingled where he'd hacked it off in retaliation. Truth told, Mia hated him like poison, and the idea of taking orders from him sat about as well with her as a collar on a cat.

Solis glowered, white eyes turned to the ceiling, his robe straining against the span of his shoulders. He dwarfed the other Ministry members, making them look like children. Mia supposed she should feel intimidated, but she found it all just another reminder of how ill-suited for his role Solis seemed.

He doesn't even fit the robe he's supposed to wear . . .

"So," Spiderkiller asked, without preamble. "Gaius Aurelius is dead?"

". . . Aye, Shahiid," Mia replied.

"Word has it you were almost killed in the process," Mouser mused.

"A scratch, Shahiid." She shrugged, wincing at the pull of the stitches in her shoulder. "Though I'll not be dancing for a while."

"You can barely walk, Acolyte," Solis growled.

"All due respect, Revered Father," Mia said, temper fraying. "But I was anointed by Lord Cassius with his dying breath. I'm not an acolyte. I'm a Blade."

Solis sneered. "That remains to be seen."

"I've four kills to my name already."

Mouser tilted his head. "Don't you mean five?"

"Surely you haven't forgotten murdering a king of the Dweymeri in his own keep without our permission?" Spiderkiller asked.

Mia bit down on her response. Glancing again at the name she'd carved into the unmarked tomb on the western wall.

TRIC.

They'd made a promise. Him to her and her to him. If she were to fall, Tric had sworn to murder Scaeva and Duomo for her. And if he fell, she swore she'd kill his wretched bastard of a grandfather, Swordbreaker. In truth, she thought she was owed a death after saving the lives of every man and woman in this room. But perhaps here was the reason she'd been sent to a backwater like Galante?

Silence rang in the hall, Mia stewing within it.

"May I ask why I am here?" she finally ventured.

Solis's lip curled. "You have a devotee, little Blade."

The girl raised an eyebrow at the Revered Father. "If it's someone in this hall, they hide it very well."

Aalea smiled, lips dark as blood. "Perhaps 'patron' is a better word. The last three offerings you performed—the son of Senator Aurelius, Magistrate Phillip Cicerii, and the mistress of Armando Tulli—were all requested by the same client of the Church. They specifically requested the services of 'she who slew the justicus of the Luminatii Legion and his finest centuries beside him.' And they paid handsomely for you."

"Who is this patron, Shahiid?"

"Irrelevant," Solis scowled. "All you need know is that, miracle of miracles, they are pleased with your results. You are being sent after bigger game."

Mia looked Solis up and down, considering. From the scowl at his brow, the tension in his jaw, she'd wager her last coin the Revered Father had violently objected to her assignment. But despite that, she'd been appointed anyway. Which meant this patron was powerful. Or rich. Or both.

Well, that narrows it down . . .

"So what new backwater does my illustrious patron send me to?" Mia asked. "Last Hope? Amai? Sto—"

"Godsgrave," Mouser replied.

Mia's tongue cleaved to her teeth, her heart running quicker.

Maw's teeth. The 'Grave . . .

The capital of Itreya. Only the Church's finest Blades served in the City of Bridges and Bones. Grand Cardinal Duomo lived there, as did Consul Scaeva. If Mia wanted revenge for her familia, her first step was getting close to the men who murdered them.

If she'd somehow lucked into a dream posting . . .

"I know your mind," Solis growled. "I know why you came to this Church and what it is you seek. So, while I am sending you to the capital against my better judgment, I am telling you this now, and I am telling you once." Solis towered over her, blind eyes boring into Mia's own. "Consul Julius Scaeva is not to be touched."

Mia scowled. "Wh—"

"I will not tolerate you pursuing your own vendettas while serving this Ministry," Solis said. "You already murdered a bara of the Dweymeri out of some misplaced sympathy for the boy you were bedding. I'll not have another unsanctioned kill wrought by your hand. Or your quim."

"Who I bed is my concern. And you don't get to dec—"

"I do decide!" Solis roared. "I am Revered Father of this congregation! I give not a beggar's cuss for who you wet the furs with, but Swordbreaker was a fucking king! What if he'd been a patron of this Church? We'd have breached Sanctity! Our reputation shattered over a child's whim."

"It wasn't a whim, it was a promise!"

"Let us speak of promises, then, girl," Solis spat. "Disobey me, and I promise you an ending from which even the Goddess herself would avert her gaze. Scaeva is not to be touched!"

"And why not?" Mia looked among the Ministry, her anger finally getting the better of her. "The Luminatii killed Lord Cassius, almost killed all of you! You think Scaeva didn't order it? Remus was a fucking lapdog. You think he took a piss without asking the consul's permission first?"

"Hear me now!" Solis raised a finger in warning, blind eyes flashing. "Scaeva will be dealt with. But in our own way. In our own time. You are a servant of Our Lady of Blessed Murder, and in the Mother's name, that means you fucking serve!"

Mia felt her cheeks flush with rage. She stared into Solis's blind eyes and imagined drawing the gravebone stiletto in her sleeve. Cutting his throat. Spilling his steaming guts onto the floor. But amid the outrage, a single, ice-cold thought took her by the scruff of the neck and shook her 'til she was still.

. . . He's right.

She had been childish.

She had risked the Church's reputation in killing Swordbreaker.

She had thought to kill Duomo and Scaeva if she got back to the 'Grave.

Her knuckles were white on the book in her grip. But she forced her fingers to unclench, speaking words that rang heavy in the quiet dark.

"In the Mother's name. I will serve."

Solis's huge frame slowly relaxed—Mia realized he was actually hoping she'd buck. But after a long heavy silence, the big man reached into his robe, produced a leather scroll case sealed with black wax.

"One kill. A woman who calls herself 'the Dona.' Leader of a braavi gang who run in the streets of Little Liis. You grew up there, neh?"

". . . Aye." Mia reached for the case.

"*One stipulation,*" *the big man said, holding up his finger.* "*An item of import to your patron. A map, written in Old Ysiiri and set with a seal shaped like a sickle's blade. The Dona is brokering an exchange with the map's current owner. You must take the map, along with her life.*"

"*. . . What's the map of?*"

"*It provides detailed directions to the Empire of None of Your Fucking Concern.*"

"*The exchange will take place in the headquarters of the Toffs,*" *Spiderkiller said.* "*Before month's end.*"

"*That's eight turns from now,*" *Mia said.*

"*Black Mother be praised,*" *Solis replied.* "*The girl can count.*"

"*On both hands, Revered Father.*"

Solis gave over the scroll case with a scowl. Mia sucked her lip, mind spinning. Eight turns wasn't long to plan a kill like this. She needed backup she could trust.

"*Can I bring my own Hand to the 'Grave?*" *she asked.* "*My last one met a crossbow bolt he didn't like.*"

"*I fear not,*" *Aalea said, as if reading her mind.* "*Naev is needed here. With most of our blood pools destroyed, our supply situation is critical. A new chapel has been built in the necropolis beneath Godsgrave. The local bishop will provide you with a Hand. Marius has already sent a blood missive informing him of your arrival.*"

Solis tilted his head, milk-white eyes aimed somewhere over Mia's shoulder.

"*You have eight turns to end this Dona and recover the map. Your patron may have more offerings for you, presuming you do not perish in pursuit of this first.*"

"*I'm too pretty to perish.*" *Mia tossed her fringe from her eyes.*

Solis sneered. "*Marielle will tend to your wounds. Marius will prepare your transportation to Godsgrave. Say your farewells and be in his chambers by midbells.*"

Questions bounced around inside her skull. Who was this patron? Why kill a member of the braavi? Why did they request her specifically? What's on this map?

It doesn't matter, she realized.

It wasn't her place to ask. It was her place to serve. The sooner she proved herself, the sooner she'd earn a permanent posting in the Godsgrave Chapel. And from there, no matter what Solis might say, she'd be one step closer to her revenge.

The wolf did not pity the lamb.

The storm begged no forgiveness of the drowned.

"*I'll not fail,*" *Mia vowed.* "*In the Black Mother's name, I swear it.*"

Solis folded his arms, his face unreadable in the gloom.

"*Go,*" *he finally said.* "*May Our Lady be late when she finds you. And when she does, may she greet you with a kiss.*"

Mia took the scroll case, tucked it under her arm along with her beaten book. Bowing low, she backed slowly out of the hall. As she stalked away down the darkened corridors, past beautiful stained-glass windows and grotesque bone sculptures, two shapes slipped from the darkness and fell into step alongside her.

A cat made of shadows. And beside it, a wolf of the same.

"Can you believe him?" Mia hissed. "Calling me 'acolyte,' the bastard."

". . . you act as if solis's bastardry is some kind of revelation . . . ," Mister Kindly replied.

Eclipse's growl came from somewhere beneath the floor.

". . . CASSIUS ALWAYS THOUGHT OF HIM AS AN ARROGANT THUG. OF ALL THE MIN-ISTRY, HE LIKED SOLIS LEAST. ONE TURN, WE SHOULD TEACH HIM A LESSON IN MAN-NERS . . ."

". . . there are less dramatic forms of suicide, pup . . ."

". . . SO LITTLE FAITH IN OUR MISTRESS, LITTLE KITTEN . . ."

". . . she is not *yours*, you w—"

"Black Mother, enough," Mia snapped, rubbing her temples. "The last thing I need to hear right now is you two bickering like a pair of old maids."

Her passengers fell quiet, leaving only a disembodied choir to echo in the dark. Mia took a deep breath, tried to pull her notorious temper into check. They were still treating her like a novice. Despite all she'd done. But if nothing else, she was headed to Godsgrave. The patronage of this mysterious benefactor was unexpected, but in truth she was glad somebody was recognizing the talent it took to murder a justicus and a hundred of his men. If it got her closer to Scaeva and Duomo, all the better.

But still, her mind swum with images of her fight in the necropolis. That thing and its gravebone blades, the tentacles writhing at the edges of its cowl. Though she couldn't find it in her to be afraid with the shadows so thick at her feet, she knew there was something grander at play here.

She looked at the book under her arm, running her fingers across the time-worn cover. The tarnished brass clasp.

"Seek the crown of the moon," she muttered.

". . . we have until midbells . . ."

The girl hooked her thumbs into her belt.

Realized she was dying for a smoke.

"Time enough to take my library books back."

Her cell smelled like piss and stale misery.

The straw was musty, the bucket in the corner crusted in filth and flies. Mia had been escorted from the Pit, Teardrinker nodding farewell as she was taken out through the gates. Four heavyset legionaries had marched her across the roiling marketplace, finally locking her in a holding pen inside a large administratii building. Though her price was settled, coin had yet to be paid. She had a few hours before her new domina took full possession. A few hours to pull together the tattered threads of her plan.

"*. . . we must inform the viper . . .*"

Mia scowled at Mister Kindly. He was only a darker shape against the shadows thrown by the bars across the floor. The cells beside Mia's were empty, but she kept her voice a whisper.

"I wish you wouldn't call her that."

"*. . . you have another term less flattering . . . ?*"

"You could use her bloody name."

The not-cat made a sniffing sound; impressive for a creature without lungs.

"*. . . we were supposed to be purchased by leonides. leonides's daughter bought you instead. the viper has no way of knowing this. she and eclipse will be waiting for us at leonides's collegium in whitekeep as planned . . .*"

"That *was* something of an oversight," Mia admitted.

"*. . . this entire plan is oversight and folly, stitched together by jiggery-fuckery . . .*"

"I know what I'm doing."

"*. . . a pity, then, that the viper does not . . .*"

Mia sighed. "You'll have to go tell her. Can you make your way to Whitekeep?"

"*. . . i am certain i can find a ship to stow aboard. but what will you do . . . ?*"

"What else can I do?" Mia shrugged. "Train in Leona's stable. Fight. Win. The destination hasn't changed, just the starting point."

"*. . . and where do i tell the viper to meet you? where is your new dona's collegium . . . ?*"

"I've no fucking idea."

"*. . . o, aye. you certainly know what you're doing . . .*"

Mia flipped the knuckles at the shadowcat, dragged her matted hair behind her ears. She was still covered in dried blood, old sweat, dust. Sitting in the straw, she tried not to picture the faces of the men she'd killed in the Pit. She'd needed to impress, and she'd done so . . . after a fashion. She'd killed dozens who'd stood in her way before now. But still, those pit fighters had only been doing as they were bid . . .

"I feel like shit," she sighed.

"*. . . you do not smell particularly pleasant either . . .*"

"That's not what I—"

". . . you cannot afford to pity those men, mia. swimming this deep, your compassion will only serve to drown you. you must be as hard and as sharp as the men you hunt . . ."

"If not for the pity I took in my final trial at the Red Church, I'd have been at the initiation feast when Ashlinn and Osrik poisoned the Ministry. We'd *all* be dead."

". . . you're just going to keep rubbing that in, aren't y—"

Footsteps echoed down the corridor, and the not-cat faded away like smoke. Mia looked up to see an administratii unlocking her cell. The man was stocky, bearded, clad in white robes marked with the three suns of the Itreyan Republic. Beside him stood a young boy in a short-sleeved novice frock, carrying a tall chair and a mahogany box.

Dona Leona walked softly into the cell, followed by one of the most well-built men Mia had ever seen. He was Itreyan, perhaps in his mid-thirties, thick beard going gray at the edges, thick hair swept up and back in a long tail. His skin was like leather, and a particularly vicious scar bisected his brow, cheek and lip, twisting his features into a perpetual scowl. His stare was bloodshot, and he leaned heavily on a walking stick, its handle shaped like a lion's head. Looking down, Mia saw he was missing his left leg below the knee, an iron pin affixed there instead.

He scowled at Mia with steel-gray eyes, his voice like cracking stone.

"She's a girl."

Dona Leona raised one perfectly manicured brow. "I noticed."

"'Byss and blood, Dona, you dropped a thousand silver on this slip? I'm not a miracle worker. I need good clay to work with."

"She killed five men in five minutes," Leona said. "She was worth every coin."

"A bloody good thing, then. Since we've not a beggar left to our names."

"We've two other purchases this trip, both fine stock. And you've no cause to rebuke me, Executus. If you weren't out drinking the Garden dry yester-eve, you'd have been with me this morn when I made purchase."

The big man grunted, looked again at Mia.

"On your feet, slave."

Mia complied mutely, stood with hands clasped. The man limped in a circle around her, iron leg clanking on the stone. He poked the muscle at her gut, squeezed her biceps with massive hands, checked her teeth. Mia endured the inspection silently, eyes downturned. She could smell goldwine on his breath.

"She's too short," he declared. "No reach in these arms."

"She is fast as the wind," Leona replied.

"She's too young. It'll be years before she's ready for the sand."

"Five men," Leona repeated, "in five minutes."

"She's a *girl*," the big man growled.

"So was I," the dona replied softly. "And you never thought lesser of me for it."

"One sniff of her and the men will lose their fucking minds."

"Did my father not say the same about me when I'd visit the collegium? And was it not you who asked that I be allowed to stay? To learn?"

"A different tale, Mi Dona. You were the domini's daughter. This slip's going to be down in the barracks with the rest of them."

"And until she proves herself in the Winnowing, you will ensure my investment comes to no harm," Leona said coolly.

"She'll never survive the Winnowing."

"Then you will have the distinct pleasure of saying 'I told you so,' Executus."

The big man scowled at Mia. She met his stare, just for a second. Fury burned in the blacks of her pupils as a silent vow echoed in her mind.

You'll be eating those words come truelight, bastard.

"What's your name?" he asked.

"They call me Crow, Mi Don," she replied, eyes once more to the floor.

"Do I look like a fucking don to you, girl? You will address me as Executus."

It was all Mia could do not to bury her knee in his bollocks. Punch his teeth loose from his jaw and dance on his head.

"Yes, Executus," she replied.

The man glowered, his expression turned all the darker by his scar. Blade-work, she reckoned. Probably earned somewhere on the sand. He moved like a fighter. Graceful and powerful, despite the missing leg.

"We sail on the morrowtide," Leona said. "The sooner we return to Crow's Nest and begin her training, the better."

Mia's heart surged in her chest.

". . . Crow's Nest?" she whispered.

The slap knocked her back into the wall. Her head cracked on the stone and she collapsed to her knees, gasping. She was back on her feet in a moment, eyes flashing with hatred as she glared at the man who'd slapped her. But quick as silver, the executus's fist crashed into her belly, sending her to her knees once more.

He's fast . . .

Mia felt a brutish hand in her hair, dragging back her head as she gasped in pain.

"You forget your place, girl," the big man said. "If ever again you speak in presence of your domina without being spoken to, I'll set my blade to your tongue and feed it to my fucking dog. Do you hear me?"

Patience . . .

"Yes, Executus," she whispered.

The man grunted, released his hold. Mia glanced up at Leona, saw the woman regarding her with a cool, imperious gaze. Whatever her opinion of Mia's martial skills, it was clear her new domina had no issue with her man's brutal methods.

After a moment's tense silence, Dona Leona turned to the administratii, still waiting patiently in the corridor.

"Come, then, be about your work."

The administratii shuffled into the cell, his novice beside him. The boy plonked the tall chair down beside Mia, opened the mahogany box he carried and proffered it to the administratii. Inside Mia saw a collection of iron needles. Powders in stoppered phials, small bottles of ink. Her shadow surged, fear swelling in her belly. She knew this was coming. It was all part of the game. But still . . .

"Sit," the administratii said.

Mia dragged herself up from the floor, glanced at the buckles and straps on the chair's armrests. They obviously intended to bind her for what came next. She knew if she spoke again, she'd only earn herself another blow. And so she fixed her stare on the small barred window, the blue sky beyond. And she remained standing.

The executus growled deep, raised his hand to strike.

"Do as you're—"

"No," Dona Leona said, watching Mia with curious eyes. "Let her stand."

"All respect, Dona Leona," said the administratii, "but this is no simple inkwerk. The process is arkemical. The pain immense. She is likely to swoon."

Mia thought back to her scourging at Weaver Marielle's hands and almost laughed at the word. That same laughter twinkled in the Dona Leona's eyes.

"A hundred silver says she does nothing of the sort."

The executus groaned softly. The administratii looked taken aback.

"I am not a gambling man, Mi Dona."

"But you *are* a man who insists on telling me what I already know?" Leona's tone turned razor-sharp. "I grew up in the finest gladiatii collegium in all the Itreyan Republic. I know how a damned slave brand works. Now proceed."

The administratii almost succeeded in stifling his sigh. He turned to the box, set about unstopping phials, mixing components into a shallow glass bowl. The poisoncrafter in Mia watched with interest, noting the way the arkemical concoction came together, bubbling and hissing and spitting black.*

The administratii dipped his needle, raised it to Mia's face. The novice stood behind her, held her head steady. The girl forced herself to be still, grit her teeth. Lining up the steel against Mia's cheek, the administratii hefted a thin jeweler's hammer. The girl held her breath. And without further foreplay, the administratii smacked the needle through Mia's cheek and straight into the bone beyond.

Black fire. Burning agony. Mia's eyes grew wide, pupils dilated, the pain lancing through her skull and stealing her breath away. Her knees buckled, black stars bursting in her eyes. The administratii stepped back, obviously expecting her to fall. But with her shadow swelling, chest heaving, the girl remained on her feet.

Mia looked at Leona. The dona was watching her with a growing smile.

"Well?" the woman asked the administratii. "Proceed!"

The man shrugged, and with no more pause for drama, began hammering the needle into Mia's cheek, over and over again. Small series of three tiny blows, each like a thunderclap in her head.

tapTAPTAP

tapTAPTAP

Fingernails digging into her palms.

White spots swelling before her eyes.

The room rolling beneath her like a ship in a storm.

tapTAPTAP

tapTAPTAP

---

*The arkemy of slave brands is a secret tightly guarded by the Itreyan administratii. The process not only marks a person's skin, but also the bone beneath, and the tattoo will bleed through scar tissue and reassert itself should the recipient decide to remove their brand through knifework or flame.

There are only four ways to remove an arkemical brand.

First, at the hands of the administratii, after one's freedom is purchased or earned. Second, by Ysiiri sorcery. Third, by hacking out pieces of one's own skull, but since wandering about with a missing cheekbone is something of a giveaway of one's fugitive status, the agony is hardly worth it. And lastly, by dying—through some rude semblance of Old Ysiiri bloodmagik, the arkemical brand is tied to the recipient's own life, and once it ends, the mark on their cheek will slowly dissolve over the course of the next few minutes.

Thus, the only freedom most slaves ever achieve is in the arms of death.

The anticipation was the worst of it. The moment between one sequence and the next. That tiny respite that seemed an eternity, waiting for the pain to begin again. Marius's scourging, Marielle's weaving . . . nothing she'd ever felt in her life had come close, made all the worse by the bitter thought that in this moment, to the world outside this cell, her life was no longer her own.

tapTAPTAP

If not for Mister Kindly, she thought she might have broken.

tapTAPTAP

But at the end
after all the pain
all the praying
cheek bleeding
legs trembling
Mia still stood.

"A good thing," Dona Leona declared, "that you are not a betting man, sir."

The administratii packed up his gear without a word. Aiming a poison glance at Mia, he gave a curt bow to the dona, and with his novice trailing behind, swept from the cell with a rustle of black cloth. Leona turned to her executus with a triumphant smile.

"You ask for clay to work with, Executus? I give you steel."

The big man looked at Mia with narrowed eyes. "Steel breaks before it bends."

"Four Daughters, you're never happy are you?" Leona sighed. "Come. We should let her rest. She will need her strength in turns to come."

The dona cupped Mia's face, wiping her wounded cheek with a gentle thumb. Sapphire-blue eyes burning into her own.

"We will bleed the sands red, you and I," she said. *"Sanguii e Gloria."*

Gifting her a final smile, Leona swept from the room in a flurry of blue silk. The executus limped after her, locked the door behind him. The clank of his iron leg faded with his dona down the corridor.

Mia sank to her knees. Her cheek was swollen, throbbing with pain. Her palms were bleeding from the press of her nails. She ran her fingertips over her skin, feeling the raised ridges of the two interlocking circles branded just below her right eye. But beneath the remembered agony, her mind was racing, the dona's words tumbling inside her skull with the echoes of the hammer blows.

They're taking me to—

". . . crow's nest . . . ?"

She glanced up at the not-cat, once more cleaning his not-paw with his not-tongue. Licking at parched lips, she tried to find her voice.

"It was the home of the Familia Corvere. *My* familia. Consul Scaeva gave it to Justicus Remus as reward for ending my father's rebellion against the Senate."

"*. . . and now leona owns it . . . ?*"

Mia shrugged mutely. The not-cat tilted his head.

"*. . . are you well . . . ?*"

Her father, holding her hand as they walked in fields of tall sunsbell flowers. Her mother standing atop battlements of ochre stone, cool wind playing in her long dark hair. Mia had grown up in Godsgrave—her father's role as justicus meant he could never stay away from the City of Bridges and Bones for long. But every few summersdeeps, they'd traveled to Crow's Nest for a week or two, just to be with one another. Those had been the happiest turns of Mia's life. Away from Godsgrave's crush, its poison politics. Her parents seemed happier there. Closer somehow. Her brother Jonnen had been born there. She remembered visits from General Antonius, the would-be king who'd hanged beside her father. He and her parents would stay up late into the night, drinking and laughing and O, so alive.

All of them gone now.

"*. . . i should go. find a ship bound for whitekeep. tell the viper to seek you in crow's nest . . .*"

"*. . . Aye,*" she nodded.

"*. . . will you be all right while i am gone . . . ?*"

The thought should have terrified her. She knew if Mister Kindly weren't there, it would have. For seven years, ever since her father died, the shadowcat had been beside her. She knew he had to leave, that she couldn't do this all by herself. But the thought of being alone, of living with the fear he usually drank to nothing . . .

"I'll be well enough," she replied. "Just don't dawdle."

"*. . . i will be swift. never fear . . .*"

She sighed. Pressed her hand to the brand on her throbbing cheek.

"And never, ever forget."

CHAPTER 6

MORTALITY

The athenaeum opened at the touch of Mia's finger, the colossal stone doors swinging wide as if they were carved of feathers. And taking a deep breath, clutching her tome to her breast, she limped out into her favorite place in the entire world.

Looking out over the mezzanine to the endless shelves below, the girl couldn't help but smile. She'd grown up inside books. No matter how dark life became, shutting out the hurt was as easy as opening a cover. A child of murdered parents and a failed rebellion, she'd still walked in the boots of scholars and warriors, queens and conquerors.

The heavens grant us only one life, but through books, we live a thousand.

"A girl with a story to tell," came a voice from behind her.

Smiling, Mia turned to see an old man standing beside a trolley piled high with books. He wore a scruffy waistcoat, two shocks of white hair trying to flee his balding scalp. Thick spectacles sat on a hooked nose, his back bent like a sickle. The word "ancient" did him as much justice as the word "beautiful" did Shahiid Aalea.

"Good turn to you, Chronicler," Mia bowed.

Without asking, Chronicler Aelius plucked his ever-present spare cigarillo from behind his ear, lit it on his own and offered it to Mia. Leaning against the wall with a wince as her stitches pulled, she puffed and sighed a shade of contented gray.

Aelius leaned beside her, his own cigarillo bobbing on his lips as he spoke.

"All right?"

"All right," she nodded.

"How was Galante?"

Mia winced again, the pain of her sutures twinging in her backside.

"A pain in the arse," she muttered.

The old man grinned around his smoke. "So what brings you down here?"

Mia held up the tome she'd brought with her across the blood walk. It was bound in stained leather, tattered and beaten. The strange symbols embossed in the cover hurt her eyes to look at and its pages were yellowed with age.

"I supposed I should return this. I've had it eight months."

"I was starting to think I'd have to send out a search party."

"That'd be unpleasant for all concerned, I'd bet."

The old man smiled. "The late fees are rather exorbitant in a library like this."

The chronicler had left the book in Mia's room, right before she was posted to Galante. In the intervening months, she'd pored over the pages more times than she could count. The pity of it was, she still didn't understand the half of it, and truth told, in recent turns, she'd become more than a little disillusioned about it. But her encounter in the Galante necropolis had renewed her interest tenfold.

The book was written by a woman named Cleo—a darkin like Mia, who spoke to the shadows just as she did. Cleo lived in a time before the Republic, and the book was a diary of sorts, detailing her journey through Itreya and beyond. It spoke of meetings between her and other darkin—meetings that ended with Cleo apparently eating her fellows. The strange thing was, from Cleo's writing, she'd encountered dozens of other darkin in her travels. And from the look of the woman's scribbled self-portraits, she was accompanied by dozens of passengers, wearing a multitude of different shapes—foxes, birds, serpents, and the like. An entire shadow menagerie at her command.

In all her life, the only darkin Mia had met was Lord Cassius. And the only two daemons were Mister Kindly and Eclipse.

So where the 'byss were the rest of them?

Amid nonsense scrawl and pictograms that spoke of her ever-growing madness, the latter half of the book concerned Cleo's search for something she called "the Crown of the Moon"—just as that shadowthing in the Galante necropolis had told Mia to do. And flipping through the illustrations after her encounter, Mia had seen several that bore an uncanny resemblance to the figure that had saved her life.

Sadly, Cleo made no mention of who or what this "Moon" might be.

The book was written in an arcane language Mia had never seen, but Mister Kindly and Eclipse were both able to read it. Strangest of all, it contained a map of the world in the time before the Republic, but the bay of Godsgrave was missing entirely. Instead, a landmass filled the sea where the Itreyan capital now stood. This peninsula was marked with an X, and an unsettling declaration:

Here he fell.

"Did you read this before you gave it to me?" Mia asked.

The old man shook his head. "Couldn't make out a bloody word. Only thing that made me think of you was the pictures. Make any sense to you?"

". . . Not half as much as I'd like."

Aelius shrugged. "You asked me to look for books on darkin, and so I did. Didn't promise you'd be any more enlightened when you were done."

"*No need to rub it in, good Chronicler.*"

Aelius smirked. "I'm always on the lookout for more. If I find anything else of interest down here, I'll send it to your chambers. But I'd not hold my breath."

Mia nodded, dragging on her smoke. Niah's athenaeum was actually a library of the dead. It contained a copy of every book that had ever been destroyed in the history of the written language. Moreover, it also held other tomes that had never been written in the first place. Memoirs of murdered tyrants. Theorems of cruci-fied heretics. Masterpieces of geniuses who ended before their time.

Chronicler Aelius had told her new books were appearing constantly, that the shelves were always shifting. And though Niah's athenaeum was a wondrous place as a result, the downside was plain: finding a particular book in here was like trying to find a particular louse in a dockside sweetboy's crotch.

"*Chronicler, have you heard of the Moon? Or any crowns said Moon might be partial to?*"

Aelius's stare turned wary.

"*Why?*"

"*You answer questions with questions an awful lot,*" *Mia sighed.* "*Why is that?*"

"*Do you remember what I said that turn you first came down here?*"

"*See, there you go again.*"

"*Do you remember?*"

"*You said I was a girl with a story to tell.*"

"*And what else?*"

Smoke drifted from the girl's lips as the old man stared her down.

"*You said maybe here's not where I'm supposed to be,*" *she finally replied.* "*Which stank like horseshit at the time, and smells even worse now. I proved myself. The Ministry would all be nailed to crosses in the 'Grave if not for me. And I'm sick and bloody tired of everybody around here seeming to forget that.*"

"*You don't find any irony in earning your place in a cult of assassins by saving half a dozen lives?*"

"*I killed almost a hundred men in the process, Aelius.*"

"*And how do you feel about that?*"

"*What are you, my nursemaid?*" *Mia snapped.* "*A killer is what I am. The wolf doesn't pity the lamb. And the—*"

"*Aye, aye, I know the tune.*"

"*And you know why I'm here. My father was executed as a traitor to entertain a mob. My mother died in a prison, and my baby brother beside her. And the men responsible need a fucking killing. That's how I feel about it.*"

The old man hooked his thumbs into his waistcoat. "*Problem with being a librarian is there's some lessons you just can't learn from books. And the problem* with being an assassin is there's some mysteries you just can't solve by stabbing fuck out of them."

"Always riddles with you," Mia growled. "Do you know about this Moon or no?"

The old man sucked on his cigarillo, looked her up and down. "I know this much. Some answers are learned. But the important ones are earned."

"O, Black Goddess, now you're a poet, too?"

The chronicler frowned, crushed his cigarillo out against the wall.

"Poets are wankers."

Aelius dropped the murdered butt of his smoke into his waistcoat. He looked down at the book in Mia's hand. Back up into her eyes.

"You can keep that. Nobody else can read it anyways."

With a small nod, he took hold of his RETURNS trolley.

"What, that's all the explanation I get?" Mia asked.

Aelius shrugged. "Too many books. Too few centuries."

The old man wheeled his trolley off into the dark. Watching him fade into the shadows, the girl took a savage drag of her cigarillo, jaw clenched.

". . . well, that was enlightening . . ."

". . . AELIUS HAS ALWAYS BEEN THAT WAY. BEING CRYPTIC MAKES HIM FEEL IMPORTANT . . ."

Mia scowled at the shadowwolf materializing beside her.

"Are you sure Lord Cassius never learned anything of this, Eclipse? He was head of the entire congregation. You're telling me he knew nothing about what it was to be darkin? Cleo? The Moon? Any of it?"

". . . I TOLD YOU, WE NEVER LOOKED. CASSIUS FOUND ENOUGH MEANING IN LIFE BY ENDING THE LIVES OF OTHERS. HE NEEDED NO MORE THAN THAT . . ."

Mister Kindly snorted. ". . . small things and small minds . . ."

". . . HAVE A CARE, LITTLE GRIMALKIN. HE WAS MY FRIEND WHEN YOU WERE STILL SHAPELESS. HE WAS AS BEAUTIFUL AS THE DARK AND AS SHARP AS THE MOTHER'S TEETH. SPEAK NO ILL OF HIM . . ."

Mia sighed, pinching the bridge of her nose. She couldn't understand how Cassius had never sought the truth of himself. She'd wondered on it since she was a child. Old Mercurio and Mother Drusilla had said she was chosen of the Goddess.

But chosen for what?

She remembered fighting in the streets of Last Hope with Ashlinn. Her attack on the Basilica Grande when she was fourteen. On both occasions, simply looking at the trinity—the holy symbol of Aa—had caused her agony. The Light God hated her. She'd felt it. Sure as the ground beneath her feet. But why? And what the 'byss did this "Moon" have to do with any of it?

And Remus.

Fucking Remus.

He was dead by her hand on a dusty Last Hope thoroughfare. His attack on the Mountain failed. His men slaughtered on the sands all around him. But before she'd plunged her gravebone blade into his throat, the justicus had uttered words that turned her entire world upside down.

"I will give your brother your regards."

Mia shook her head.

But Jonnen is *dead.* Mother told me so.

So many questions. Mia could taste frustration mixed with the smoke on her tongue. But her answers were in Godsgrave. And Black Mother be praised, that was exactly *where this mysterious patron of hers was sending her.*

Time to stop moaning and start moving.

Mia limped out from the athenaeum. Down the winding stair toward the Church's belly. Through the puddles of stained-glass light, Mister Kindly on her shoulder and Eclipse prowling before her. The Church choir rang as they trod the winding stairs, the long and twisting halls, until finally, they reached Weaver Marielle's chambers.

She took a breath, rapped on the heavy door. It opened after a moment, and Mia found herself looking into scarlet eyes, down to a beautiful, bloodless smile.

"Blade Mia," Marius said.

The Blood Speaker was clad in his indecent britches and red silk robe, open as ever at his chest. The room beyond was lit by a single arkemical lamp, the walls adorned with hundreds of different masks, all shapes and sizes. Death masks and children's masks and Carnivalé masks. Glass and ceramic and papier-mâché. A room of faces, without a single mirror in sight.

"Thou art here for a weaving," Marius said.

"Aye," Mia nodded, meeting those blood-red eyes without fear. "Wounds heal in time, but I'll not have much of it where I'm headed."

"The City of Bridges and Bones," the speaker mused. "No place more dangerous in all the Republic."

"You've not seen my laundry basket," Mia replied.

Marius smirked, glanced over his shoulder.

"Sister love, sister mine? Thou hast company."

Mia saw a misshapen form shuffle into the arkemical glow. The woman was albino pale like her brother, but what little Mia could see of her skin was swollen and cracked, blood and pus leaking through the bandages about her hands and face. She was clad in a black velvet robe, her lips splitting as she looked at Mia and smiled.

"Blade Mia," Marielle whispered.

"Weaver Marielle," Mia said, bowing.

"To the 'Grave she goes. At Father Solis's word, to a new patron's arms. And though stitched, still she bleeds." Marius shivered slightly. "I smell it on her."

"All thy hurts shall be mended, little darkin," Marielle lisped. "Sure and true."

The weaver nodded to the dreaded stone slab that dominated her room. It was set with leather straps and buckles of polished steel—though Marielle could weave flesh like clay and mend almost any wound, the process itself was agony. Mia hated the thought of being bound for the process, truth told. Trussed up like some hog at the spit, britches around her ankles. But, resigning herself to the pain, feeling the shadows within her shadow drink down her fear, Mia limped into the chamber.

As he closed the door behind her, Speaker Marius caught her arm.

Mia looked up into his glittering eyes, snow-pale lashes. He leaned close, closer, and for a terrible, thrilling moment, she thought he might kiss her. But instead, Marius spoke with lowered voice, lips brushing her ear, barely a whisper.

"Two lives ye saved, the turn the Luminatii pressed their sunsteel to the Mountain's throat. Mine, and my sister love's. Marielle's debt to thee was repaid the turn she gave Naev back her face. But my debt, little Blade, is still owed. Know this, in nevernights to come. As deep and dark as the waters ye swim might turn, on matters of blood, count upon a speaker's vow, ye may."

Marius fixed her in his scarlet stare, voice as sharp as the gravebone at her wrist.

"Blood is owed thee, little Crow," he whispered. "And blood shall be repaid."

Mia glanced to Marielle. Back up into Marius's glittering red eyes. Her mind swimming with thoughts of Godsgrave. Braavi. Stolen maps and hidden patrons and a Ministry that seemed to feel nothing but ire toward her.

". . . Do you know something that I don't, Speaker?"

A beautiful, bloodless smile was her only reply. With a swish of his scarlet robe, Speaker Marius motioned to his sister. Mia turned to the Room of Faces and its mistress, looming above that awful slab. Marielle beckoned her with twisted fingers.

No matter what was to come, it was too late to turn back now.

And heaving a sigh, Mia lay down on the stone.

She almost wept when she saw it.

It rose from the clifftops and pierced the sky, ochre stone bleeding through to gold in the light of two burning suns. A keep carved out of the cliffs themselves, once home to one of the twelve finest familia of the Republic.

Crow's Nest.

Mia knelt on the deck of the *Gloryhound* and stared, overcome with memories. Walking in the bustling port, hand in hand with her mother. The shop-keeps calling her "little dona" and bringing her sweets. Her father striding the battlements above the ocean, sea breeze playing in his hair as he stares across the waves. Dreaming, perhaps, of the rebellion that would be his undoing.

She'd been too young to understand, too small to—

Crack!

The whip snapped across her shoulder blades, bright red pain tearing her from her reverie.

"I gave no permission for you to stop! Chin to the boards!"

Mia risked a hateful glance at the executus, looming over her with a long stock whip in hand. Sweat was dripping down her face, hair clinging to her skin. A second strike across her back was her reward for her hesitation. Arms burning with fatigue, she dropped into another push-up and rose again. Black spots swum in her eyes. The two men beside her did the same, grunting with exertion.

The journey from the Hanging Gardens had taken almost three weeks. Every turn, she and the two other slaves Leona had purchased at market were taken up on deck and run through exercises, and the sound of the executus's stock whip was starting to haunt her dreams.

Her first comrade in captivity was a hard Liisian boy named Matteo. He looked a few years older than Mia, with softly curling hair, strong arms and a pretty smile. Despite his impressive physique, Matteo had been sick as a dog for the first week they'd been at sea—Mia guessed he'd never set foot on a ship in his life.

Her second bedfellow was a burly Itreyan named Sidonius. He was in his late twenties and looked hard as a coffin nail. Bright blue eyes and a shaven head. He seemed the meaner of the pair, and looked at Mia like he wanted to fuck and/or kill her. She wasn't quite sure in which order. She wasn't sure Sidonius was either. Strangest of all, the man had a rough brand that looked to have been burned into his skin with a red-hot blade. A single word, carved right across his chest.

COWARD.

He offered no explanation for it, and Mia didn't like him enough to ask.

After another thirty-two push-ups, the executus signaled the three to stop, and Mia collapsed face-first onto the deck, arms trembling.

"Your upper body strength is a jest," the big man growled at her. "And yet, my lips are absent laughter."

"Enough for the turn, Executus," called Dona Leona from her seat on the foredeck. "They'll need to be able to walk when they meet their new familia."

"On your feet."

Mia stood slowly, staring out at the ocean. The welts on her back tickled with the sting of her sweat. The executus's salt-and-pepper hair whipped about in the ocean breeze, his beard bristling as he glared. Long minutes ticked by in silence, only the calls of gulls and the sounds of the distant port for company.

"Drink," the executus finally grunted.

Mia turned and practically dashed for the water barrel lashed to the main mast. The big Itreyan, Sidonius, shoved her aside with a curse, snatching up the ladle and drinking his fill. Mia seethed, half-tempted to knock the thug on his arse as she waited her turn, but the sensible part of her brain counseled patience. When Sidonius finished drinking, Matteo flashed her his pretty smile, waved to the barrel.

"After you, Mi Dona."

Crack!

The boy winced as the executus's whip found his back.

"I gave no permission for you to speak!"

The boy grit his teeth, bowed apology. Mia nodded thanks, turned to the water barrel, gulping down mouthful after sweet mouthful.

It chafed her almost to screaming, bowing down to these people. Told when to eat, when to drink, when to shit. The executus's contempt for them was matched only by Dona Leona's ambivalence. On the one hand, the woman treated them with a sort of affection, and spoke of the glory to come on the sands of the *venatus*. But on the other, she had them whipped for the smallest slight. They weren't allowed to look her in the eye. They spoke only when spoken to. Performing on command.

Like favored dogs, Mia realized.

Mia's parents had slaves when she was a little girl—every noble *familia* in the Republic did. But Mia's nanny, Caprice, was practically treated like blood, and her father's majordomo, a Liisian named Andriano Varnese, stayed on to serve the justicus even after he'd purchased his freedom.*

---

*In marrowborn houses and some well-established places of business, it is not uncommon for slaves to be paid for their labor—the notion being, a slave with the ability to buy back their freedom with enough hard work will work fucking hard indeed.

The rate of pay is totally unregulated, however, and many slaves earn a pittance. Unscrupulous masters will often charge a slave for their upkeep and deduct the cost from their "earnings," with the result that a lifetime of labor will not earn back the sum paid for their initial purchase.

Unfair? Absolutely. But if the system were fair, it wouldn't be much of a system, gentlefriends.

Even on the run for her life as a child, even sworn into the service of the Black Mother, Mia had never really understood what it was to not belong to herself. The thought of it burned her, like the memory of that needle being hammered into her skin. Again and again. The indignity. The shame.

But you cannot win if you do not play.

The *Gloryhound* dropped anchor in the harbor, and a short row later, Mia stood with her fellow captives on the bustling docks of the cityport beneath Crow's Nest, known as Crow's Rest. Her wrists were manacled and chafed, her clothes filthy, her hair a matted mess. Mister Kindly's absence was a knife wound in her belly, bleeding all the warmth right out of her. She looked down to her shadow, once dark enough for two, even three. Now, no different than any other around her. Fear hovered about her on black wings, and for the first time in a long time, she had to face it alone.

What if she failed?

What if she wasn't strong enough?

What if this gambit was just as foolish as Mister Kindly had warned?

"Move!" came the cry, punctuated by the sting of knotted leather on her back.

Gritting her teeth, as was now the custom, Mia did as she was told.

A wagon ride later, she was trundling into the courtyard of Crow's Nest, heart aching inside her chest. The keep seemed so familiar, the sights, the sounds, Black Mother, even the smells were unchanged. But decorating the ochre stone of the courtyard walls where the Crow of Corvere once flew, she saw the familia crest of Marcus Remus—a red falcon on a crossed black-and-white field.

I have a decidedly sinking feeling about this . . .

Memories of her childhood were awash in her head, mingled with images of her parents' end. Her father executed along with General Antonius before a howling mob. Her mother and brother dead in the Philosopher's Stone. Some part of her had always known this castle was no longer hers, that her home was not her home. But to see that bastard Remus's colors still on the walls, even after she'd buried him . . . she felt as if the whole world were shifting beneath her feet. A sickness swelled in her belly, greasy and rolling. And still, she had no time to muse on the end of her old familia.

Her new one was waiting for her.

They stood in a row, like legionaries awaiting inspection. Thirteen men and two women, dressed in loincloths and piecemeal leather armor—spaulders, padded shin guards, and the like. Sweat-soaked skin gleamed in the light of two burning suns, giving them the look of statues cast in bronze. Men and women who fought on the sands of the *venatus,* who lived and died to the cheers of a blood-drunk crowd.

Gladiatii.

As Dona Leona climbed down from the wagon, each of them slammed a fist to their chest and roared as one.

"Domina!"

Leona pressed her fingers to her lips, blew them kisses.

"My Falcons." She smiled. "You look *magnificent.*"

The executus cracked his whip, barked at Mia and her fellows to get out of the wagon. Sidonius pushed his way out first as usual. Matteo again smiled, motioned she should go before him. Mia climbed down onto the dirt, felt fifteen sets of eyes appraising her every inch. She saw lips curl, eyes narrow in derision. But the gladiatii were as disciplined as any soldier, and none breathed a word in the presence of their mistress.

"I will leave you to introductions, Executus," Dona Leona said. "I have an appointment with a ledger and a very long, very deep bath."

"Your whisper, my will," the big man bowed.

The woman disappeared beneath a tall stone archway and into the keep beyond. Mia's eyes followed, watching the way she spoke with the servants, the way she moved. The girl was reminded a little of her mother. Leona w—

Crack!

The snap of the executus's lash caught her full and complete attention.

The big man stood before them, whip in one hand. In the other, he held a handful of ochre earth from the ground at his feet, slowly letting it trickle through his fingers. He looked Mia and the other newcomers in the eye, spoke with a voice like breaking rock.

"What do I hold in my hand?"

Mai saw the ruse right away. Felt it in the hungry eyes of the gladiatii assembled behind the executus. She was new to this game, but not fool enough to fall for—

"Sand, Executus," said Matteo.

Crack!

The whip flashed across the air between them, left a bleeding welt across Matteo's chest. The boy staggered, his pretty face twisted in pain. The assembled gladiatii sneered as one.

Mia studied the fighters, assessing each in turn. The eldest couldn't be more than twenty-five. Each wore the twin interlocking circles of a fighter's slave-mark branded into their cheek. Each was a stunning physical specimen—all hard muscle and gleaming skin. But apart from that, they were each as different as iron and clay.

She saw a Dweymeri woman, with saltlocks so long they almost touched the floor. Her tattoos, which normally marked a Dweymeri's face, covered her entire body, flowing over her deep brown skin like black waterfalls. A Vaanian girl around Mia's age stood beside her, blond topknot and bright green eyes. She was barefoot, almost slight compared to her fellows. Mia looked to these women to see if she'd sense some sort of kinship or sympathy, but both stared through her as if she were made of glass.

"What do I hold in my hand?" Executus repeated.

Mia remained silent, that sickness swelling in her belly. She doubted there was a right answer, or that the executus would acknowledge it even if it was given. And she was sure one of the two she'd rode in with were stupid enough to—

"Glory, Executus," said Sidonius.

Crack!

The assembled gladiatii chuckled as Sidonius dropped to the floor, clutching split and bloody lips. Executus could wield that whip like a Caravaggio fighter wielded a rapier, and he'd gifted the big Itreyan a blow right across his fool mouth.

"You are nothing," Executus growled. "Unworthy to lick the shit from my boot. What do you know of glory? It is a hymn of sand and steel, woven by the hands of legends and sung by the roaring crowd. Glory is the province of gladiatii. And you?" His lip curled. "You are naught but a common slave."

Mia turned her eyes back to the line, studying the men behind their smiles.

They were a motley bunch, all of them bears. A handsome blonde caught her attention—he looked so similar to the Vaanian girl, they were almost certainly kin. She saw a huge Dweymeri man, his beard plaited the same as his saltlocks, his beautiful facial tattoos marred by his brand. A burly Liisian with a face like a dropped pie rocked on his heels as if unable to stand still. And standing first in the row, she saw a tall Itreyan man.

Belly turning cold.

Breath catching in her chest.

Long dark hair flowed about his shoulders, framing a face so fine it might've been sculpted by the weaver herself. He was fit and hard, but lither than some of his fellows, the whisper of a frightening speed coiled in the taut lines of his arms, the rippling muscle at his abdomen. He wore a thin silver torc about his neck—the only jewelry among the multitude. But when Mia looked into his dark, burning eyes, she felt the illness in her belly swell, innards growling as if she were suddenly, desperately hungry.

I've felt this before . . .

When she stood in the presence of Lord Cassius, the Prince of Blades . . .

Executus turned to the assembled warriors, let the sand spill from his fingers.

"Gladiatii," he asked. "What do I hold in my hand?"

Each man and woman roared as one.

"Our lives, Executus!"

"Your lives." The man turned back to the newcomers, hurling his fistful of sand to the ground. "And worthless as they be, one turn they may be sung of as legend.

"I care not what you were before. Beggars or dons, bakers or sugargirls. That life is *over*. And now, you are less than nothing. But if you watch like bloodhawks and learn what I teach, then one turn, you may stand among the chosen, upon the sands of the *venatus*. As gladiatii! And *then*"—he pointed at the bleeding Sidonius with his whip—"then, you may learn the taste of glory, pup. Then you may know the song of your pulse as the crowd roars your name, as they do Furian, the Unfallen, primus of the Venatus Tsana and champion of the Remus Collegium!"

"Furian!" The gladiatii roared as one, raising their fists and turning to the tall Itreyan standing first in the line.

The raven-haired man still stared at Mia, unblinking.

"Gladiatii fear no death!" Executus continued, spittle on his lips. "Gladiatii fear no pain! Gladiatii fear but one thing—the everlasting shame of defeat! Mark my lessons. Know your place. Train until you bleed. For if you bring such shame upon this collegium, upon your domina, I swear by almighty Aa and all four of his holy fucking Daughters, you will rue the turn your mother shit you from her belly."

He turned to his fighters, fist in the air, scar twisting his face as he roared.

"Sanguii e Gloria!"

"Blood and glory!"

The gladiatii answered as one, thumping their fists against their chests.

All except one.

The champion they called Furian.

The man was looking right at Mia, fury or lust or something in between in his stare. Her breath came quicker, skin prickling as if she were freezing. Hunger churned inside her, her mouth dry as dust, her thighs aching with want.

Mia looked to the ground at his feet, saw his shadow was no darker than the rest. But she knew this feeling, sure as she knew her own name.

And looking into his eyes, she knew he felt it too.

This man is darkin . . .

HUNGERS

A thudding heartbeat. A sea of red. A rush of vertigo, filling her head.

Mia burst from the blood pool, rising to her feet. The hurts in her shoulder and backside were mended, but she still lost her footing, saved only by the two Hands beside her. The pair helped Mia up, holding one arm apiece until they knew she was steady. Mia spat the blood off her tongue, pawed the gore from her eyes with a sigh.

Looking about, she found herself in a triangular pool brimming with blood— identical to the one she'd just left in the Quiet Mountain. The walls were patterned with sorcerii glyphs, and a map of Godsgrave was painted on the wall in blood. The archipelago sprawled across the stone, shattered isles run through with traceries of canals, looking for all the world like a headless giant laid upon its back.

Mia took a deep breath, found her feet, slung her bloody hair over her shoulder.

"Maw's teeth, I'll never get used to this," she croaked.

"Stop whining, Corvere. It beats the britches off traveling by ship."

Mia's stomach flipped as she recognized the voice. Turning to the head of the pool, she found a slender redhead staring back at her. The girl was around her age, but taller, sharper. Her eyes were green, twinkling with a feral, hunter's cunning. Her face was lightly freckled, arms folded inside the voluminous sleeves of a long black robe.

A Hand's robe.

Mia would recognize her anywhere—the girl who'd been a thorn in her side all throughout her training at the Quiet Mountain. The girl who blamed Mia's father for the death of her own. The girl who'd vowed to kill her.

"Jessamine," Mia breathed, climbing out of the pool on unsteady legs.

The redhead inclined her head. "Welcome to the City of Bridges and Bones."

"You were posted to Godsgrave?" Mia asked. "After initiation?"

"Brilliant observation, Corvere," the redhead replied. "What gave it away?"

Mia simply stared, the shadows beneath her seething. Jessamine looked her up and down, threw a bundle of linen at Mia's chest.

"Baths are this way."

The bundled fabric was a robe, and Mia dragged it around her blood-sodden body, leaving sticky red footprints as she followed Jessamine down a twisting hallway. The temperature was stifling, the stench of iron and gore almost overpowering.

Mia saw the walls and ceiling were made of thousands upon thousands of human bones. Femurs and ribs, spines and skulls, forming a dark maze run thick with shadows—whoever thought to construct the new chapel to Our Lady of Blessed Murder inside Godsgrave's vast necropolis obviously had a deep appreciation of the value of ambience. Dim light was provided by arkemical globes, held in skeletal hands on the walls. But despite being surrounded by the remains of untold thousands, Mia's eyes were fixed on the girl in front of her. Spitting the greasy blood off her tongue, she watched Jessamine as if the girl were about to sprout a second head.

After initiation, Mia knew Jessamine had been anointed as a Hand, but she'd been so caught up in her work in Galante that she'd never found out where. It seemed of all cities in the Republic, her old nemesis had been sent to work in Godsgrave.

Fucking typical . . .

The hallway ended at a door made entirely of spines, which Jessamine opened with a gentle touch. Mia saw three baths beyond, the air hung faint with ashwood smoke and honeysuckle perfume. Mia scratched at the drying blood on her face, eyes never leaving the redhead's. Marius's cryptic warning echoing in her head. The gravebone blade she kept ever strapped to her forearm was just a flick of the wrist away.

"I'll be out here." Jessamine nodded to the baths. "Don't take too long. The bishop is waiting, and he's of a darker mood than usual."

Mia stood her ground, staring into the redhead's eyes.

"You're wondering if I'm going to try to drown you, aye?" Jessamine's lips twisted in a smile. "Put a knife in you as soon as your back is turned?"

"What makes you think I'm going to turn my back, Red?"

Jessamine shook her head, her voice hard and cold.

"There's still blood between you and me. But the turn I come for you, you won't be naked in a tub with soap in your eyes. You'll be wide awake, blade in hand. I promise you that." Jessamine smiled, ear to ear. "So never fear, Corvere."

Mia looked to the steaming baths. Down to the shadow at her feet. And then she smiled back.

"I never do."

A n hour later, Mia was standing outside the chambers of the bishop of the Godsgrave Chapel. She was dressed in knee-high boots and black leathers, a doublet of crushed black velvet, hair neatly combed. Her father's gravebone longsword hung at her side, her mother's stiletto sheathed inside her ruffled sleeve.

The bishop's chambers were hidden away in a twist of bone tunnels—the chapel's innards were a labyrinth, and Mia had lost her bearings quickly. If not for Jessamine, she doubted she'd be able to find her way back to the blood pool again, which made her all the warier about being in the girl's presence.

The chamber door opened silently, and a slender young man stepped out into the shadows of the hall, dressed in dark velvet. His face had been woven since last Mia saw him, but he was still too thin, and Mia would recognize those piercing blue eyes anywhere. Dark hair, ghost-pale, lips slightly pursed against his toothless gums.

"Hush," Mia smiled.

The boy stopped, looked Mia up and down as if surprised to see her. A small smile curled his lips as he signed to her in Tongueless.

hello

She signed back, hands moving quickly.

you serve here? in godsgrave?

Hush nodded.

eight months

it's good to see you

is it

we should have a drink

The boy looked at Jessamine, then gave a noncommittal shrug.

"Listen, I hate to break up this heartwarming reunion," Jess said. "But honestly, I'm about to start weeping at the emotion, and the bishop is waiting."

Hush nodded, looked to Mia.

mother watch over you

With a small bow, the boy pressed his fingertips together and walked away down the hall, silent as a shadow. Mia watched him go, a touch saddened. She'd been an acolyte with Hush. He'd helped her in her final trials, and in turn, she'd saved his life during the Luminatii attack. But as ever, the strange boy held himself distant.

A killer first, and always.

Jess knocked on the door three times.

"*Fucksakes, what?" demanded a haggard voice from within.*

Jessamine opened the door, motioned Mia inside. The girl entered the bishop's chamber, looked about the room. Bone walls were lined with bookshelves, laden with haphazardly stacked paperwork. Sheaves of vellum and scrolls in boxes or simply piled atop one another, hundreds of books stacked without care or scattered across the floor—it looked like a globe of wyrdglass had exploded inside a drunkard's library. Along one wall was a row of weaponry from all corners of the Republic: a Luminatii sunsteel blade; a Vaanian battleaxe; a double-edged gladius from some gladiatii arena; a rapier of Liisian steel. All gleaming in the low arkemical light.

Seated at a broad wooden desk, almost hidden behind a tottering pile of paperwork, Mia saw the bishop of Godsgrave, a quill held between his liver-spotted fingers.

"*Maw's teeth," she breathed. ". . . Mercurio?"*

The old man looked up from his paperwork, pushed his spectacles up his nose. His shock of thick gray hair seemed to have gotten unrulier since she last saw him, ice-blue eyes framed by his perpetual scowl. He obviously hadn't slept well in months.

"*Well, well," Mercurio smirked. "I thought you were the Quiet One, come back to complain some more. How do, little Crow?"*

Mia looked at her former mentor with astonishment.

"*What the 'byss are you doing here?"*

"*What's it bloody look like?"*

"*They made you bishop of Godsgrave?"*

Mercurio shrugged. "Bishop Thalles got ventilated when the Luminatii purged the city. Fuckers never hit the Curio Shop for some reason, but I couldn't ever risk going back there. So, once the chapel got rebuilt, Lady Drusilla lured me out of retirement. Without the shop, I had bugger all else to do."

"*Why didn't you tell me?"*

"*You were in Galante. And in case your bloody eyes have stopped working, I've been a trifle busy. So, without further foreplay, Marius sent missive you'd be arriving. You got the particulars?"*

Mia was a little taken aback. Mercurio had never quite gotten over the fact that she'd failed her final trial. Though he'd always be fond of her, he still seemed . . . disappointed somehow. Like everyone else in the Ministry, her old master could carry a grudge. It saddened her, no doubt—the old man had taken her in, looked after her for six long years. Though she'd admit it to no one, she loved the old bastard.

But still, she was a Blade and he was now her bishop, and his tone reminded her sharply where she was. Mia produced the scroll case Solis had given her. It was leather, so it could cross the blood walk—nothing that hadn't once known the pulse of life could travel via Marius's magiks. Mia watched Mercurio unroll the parchment, pore over it with narrowed eyes.

"The Dona," he murmured.

"Leader of the Toffs," Mia replied. "They run down by the Bay of Butchers."

The bishop nodded, picked up the character sketch of Mia's mark. It showed a woman with a dark scowl, darker eyes. She wore a frock coat of a fine cut, hair styled into artful ringlets, as was the fashion among marrowborn ladies in recent seasons. A monocle was propped (rather ridiculously, Mia thought) on her right eye.

Mercurio dropped the parchment on his desk.

"Shame to bury a knife that sharp." The old man took a long sip of his tea. This close, Mia could smell the goldwine in it. "Right. The particulars are detailed, you know where to start looking. You've got eight turns to end her and snaffle this map, and the hourglass is running. What do you need from me?"

"A place to sleep. Wyrdglass. Weapons. A Hand who knows the 'Grave as well as me and can move as fast as I do."

"You've got your Hand, she's standing right behind you."

Mia turned to look at Jessamine. Back to Old Mercurio. The bishop was obviously unaware of the enmity that lay between the girls, and to bring it up seemed on the south side of petty. But Mia trusted Jessamine like she trusted the suns not to shine, and enjoyed her company the way eunuchs enjoy looking at naughty lithographs.

How best to broach this . . .

"Perhaps there's someone with more . . . experience?"

Mercurio peered at Mia over his spectacles, his expression sour.

"Blade Mia. Godsgrave is the only Red Church chapel we've managed to rebuild in the eight months since the Luminatii attack. Thanks to Grand Cardinal Duomo and his god-bothering shitheels, I'm one of two bishops servicing the whole fucking Republic, in fact, and with Scaeva running for a fourth term as consul and Godsgrave politics all aflutter, there's no end of bastards who need killing. So, given that I'm busier than a whorehouse running a two-for-one special, do me the honor of saying thank you, and taking what you're bloody given."

Mia looked her former mentor in the eye. She recognized his tone—the same one he'd use when she was a little girl and he'd caught her stealing his cigarillos. She glanced over her shoulder at Jessamine. Softly sighed.

"Thank you, Bishop."

"My fucking pleasure."

"May the Moth—"

"Aye, aye, black kisses all around. Now sod off, will you?"

Mia backed out of the room with a bow, trying not to take Mercurio's mood too personally. He'd always been a sour old cur, and running the Godsgrave Chapel at a time like this couldn't be doing his humors any favors.

Jessamine led Mia down a twisting passage, the Blade following close on her heels. Once they were safely out of the bishop's earshot, Mia took Jessamine by the arm, turned the Hand to face her.

"Are we going to have problems, you and I?"

"Whatever do you mean, Corvere?"

"I mean it's no secret we hate each other like fucking poison. But you're my Hand now. I need to be able to trust you, Jess."

The redhead's green eyes sparkled as she spoke.

"I don't like you, Corvere. You think you're clever. You think you're special. *You poisoned Diamo and cheated me out of my spot as top of Songs. But I serve the Mother, I serve the Ministry, same as you. Don't question my devotion again."*

The redhead turned and stalked off into the dark.

The shadows at Mia's feet rippled, a cold whisper in her ear.

". . . you always had a talent for making friends . . ."

". . . WELL *I* AM QUITE FOND OF YOU, IF THAT MAKES A DIFFERENCE . . ."

". . . thank the mother i am not actually capable of vomiting . . ."

". . . SHUT UP . . ."

". . . such a witty riposte . . ."

". . . WIT IS WASTED ON THE WITLESS . . ."

"If you two are quite finished?" Mia asked.

". . . mongrel . . . ," *came a soft whisper.*

". . . CUR . . . ," *came a softer reply.*

Mia folded her arms, tapping her toe on the stone. Silence fell in the corridor, punctuated only by Jessamine's receding footfalls.

"Hurry up, Corvere," the Hand called. "The hourglass isn't getting any fuller."

Thumbs in belt, Mia had no choice but to follow Jessamine down the hall.

D*arkin . . .*

Mia stared across the courtyard at the gladiatii called Furian. The man met her stare, warm breeze blowing his long dark hair about his face. His eyes burned right through her with an intensity that . . .

Well, truth told, without Mister Kindly at her side, it frightened her.

But Black Mother, what might this mean? Mia had only met one of her kind before now, and Lord Cassius had died before he gave her any answers about who or what she was. Perhaps Furian knew something more? Perhaps he held all th——

The executus cracked his whip.

"Gladiatii! Return to training!" He turned to Mia, Sidonius and Matteo. "You three. Attend me."

The gladiatii fell out, holding perfect formation as they marched down to the courtyard at the building's rear. The executus limped after them, leaning on his lion-headed cane. As Mia followed, she saw him take a sip from a metal flask at his belt.

In the rear yard, where Mia's father had once kept a stable of proud horses, she saw the grounds had been completely refitted. The ochre sands were set with training dummies, racks of shields and wooden weapons. The ground was uneven, scaffolds and pits dividing the space into different levels, from ten feet high to ten feet deep. A broad circle was marked with white stones, and sigils of the Familia Remus flew proudly upon the battlements.

The gladiatii paired off to spar. Mia saw different combinations of weapons, different fighting styles. The Vaanian girl hefted an ironwood bow and began peppering targets at the other end of the yard. Furian took up twin swords, began beating one of the training dummies as if it had insulted his mother.

The executus limped to the verandah, greeting a huge dog sitting in the shade. It was a mastiff, male, with dark fur and a studded collar. The dog was clearly overjoyed, and the big man knelt with a wince so it could slobber on his face.

"Good to see you again, old friend," he murmured, patting the dog. "Been guarding the collegium while I was gone?"

Mia and her fellows sweated in the boiling suns while Executus finished making a fuss of the dog. It was the first time she'd seen the bastard smile in a month, though with that scar at his face, it was still a little hard to tell. Once he was done, Executus limped out into the stone circle, snapped his fingers.

"Maggot," he barked. "Sword and board."

Mia caught movement from the corner of her eye, saw a girl dash out from the shade of a small building in the corner of the yard. She was Liisian; skinny and tanned, with dark hair growing wild. She couldn't have been more than twelve, but three arkemical circles branded on her cheek marked her as the highest tier of slave.

What skill is a girl that age prized for?

The girl ran to the weapon racks, picked up a wooden practice blade and a broad oaken shield, fetched them to the executus. The big man pointed the blade at Matteo.

"Come. Show me what you're made of, boy. Maggot, fetch the lad a cock and something to hide behind."

The girl nodded, ran back to the racks and returned with another wooden sword and shield. Matteo squared up, adopted a halfway-decent fighting stance.

"Attack!" Executus roared.

Matteo swung his wooden blade with a cry, but the executus blocked the assault with ease.

"I didn't ask for a fucking kiss, I said attack!"

The boy scowled, launching a series of blows, head, chest, belly. The executus was strong as a bull, but he moved slow on that iron leg of his, and Matteo's footwork proved surprisingly good. The boy pushed the older man back, sword cracking against sword, dust rising from their shields as they clashed. Mia noted the gladiatii were only sparring half-heartedly, watching the bout with interest.

Matteo grew more aggressive—like Mia, he'd obviously expected the executus to be a master bladesman. But in the face of the boy's furious attacks, Executus was on full defense. Matteo landed blow after blow against the big man's guard, utterly dominating, until the executus was pressed against the circle's edge.

And then, like a bear too early from its slumber, the man came awake.

He shifted from back to front foot in the blink of an eye, moving swift and graceful despite his iron leg. And in the space of a few seconds, he'd knocked the sword from Matteo's hand, cracked his blade into the lad's gut, and left him sprawled in the dust.

Executus loomed over the gasping boy, only a thin sheen of sweat on his brow.

"What did you learn?"

Matteo grasped his bruising belly, too breathless to speak.

"The sand is no place for brawlers," Executus said, his scar creased in a scowl. "It is a checkered board. And on it, we play the greatest game of all. A wily opponent may feign weakness. Allow you to exert yourself and learn your patterns, all without breaking a sweat. Overconfidence has ended a thousand fools who'd name themselves gladiatii. Mark this, or it will be the end of *you*. Now get off my fucking sand."

Executus turned to Mia, pointed his wooden blade.

"You next, girl. Show me how many of those thousand priests you're worth."

The girl named Maggot handed Mia a practice blade and shield with a shy smile. But Sidonius snatched the weapon from the little girl's hand, shoved Mia aside.

"Fuck that," he growled. "No bitch steps onto the sand before me."

Perhaps it was the heat, or three weeks of eating shit from this man at sea. Perhaps her legendary temper coming out to play without Mister Kindly to keep her in check, or Furian's dark eyes following her across the yard. Whatever the reason, Mia found her hands on the big man's shoulders, and her knee buried in his bollocks.

"Bitch, am I?" she whispered.

Sidonius's eyes bulged as he doubled up. Mia locked her fingers behind his head and brought his face down into her knee. She was on top of him in a heartbeat, fists pounding his jaw, teeth clenched, blood in her—

Crack!

The whip etched a line of agony across her shoulder blades. Another blow sent her scrambling away with a gasp, twisting out of range. Laughter rang among the assembled gladiatii. Executus glared at her, lash unfurled in his hand.

"That is your domina's property you just damaged, cur. If he falls now in the Winnowing, will you pay her the forfeit of his life?"

Mia rubbed the welt on her shoulder, growling. "No man speaks to me that way."

"He is not a man!" Executus spat. "He is a *slave*. As are you. And *both* of you forget your places. Until you survive the Winnowing at next *venatus,* you are less than nothing. Now pick up those weapons and show me a scrap of the promise your domina sees in you, before you truly test my patience."

The girl called Maggot helped Sidonius to his feet, and with gentle hands, led the him out of the circle. Executus coiled his lash at his belt, took another swig from his flask as Mia scooped up the sword and shield with a black scowl. Fury burned in her belly, teeth clenched tight. Mia could feel Furian watching her with those dark glittering eyes, that hunger and sickness coiled in her gut.

And without a word, she struck.

Her attacks were vicious, blinding. Dancing across the ochre sands, sliding between the executus's blows. But during her training in the mountain, she'd spent most of her time learning Caravaggio style, fighting with a sword in each hand. It wasn't likely a Blade of the Mother would be traipsing about with a great bloody shield strapped to her arm, and so in all her time, Mia had never trained how to use one.

It was deadweight. Each impact jarring her elbow, her shoulder. And as desperate to make an account of herself as she was, she was still aware enough to know that the executus was toying with her. Letting her dodge and weave and grow wearier by the moment, all the while studying her patterns and setting her up for the kill.

But she was no worthless punching bag or training dummy. She'd be damned if she let him treat her like one. And so, looking to show this man what she was truly capable of, she narrowed her eyes and reached out to the shadows at his feet.

None would have marked it—the executus's shadow barely rippled. Mia couldn't quite grasp the iron peg; the suns out here were too bright, her grip on the shadows too weak. But she held the sole of his boot well enough, just as she'd done in the Pit and the Mountain and a hundred times before. The executus's eyes widened as his stance failed him. Mia swung at his throat, tightening her hold on the shadows and fixing to teach this man who thought her less than nothing exactly what she was worth.

And then she lost her grip.

The shadows slithered from her hold like sand through her fingertips, releasing the big man's boot. Executus slammed his shield into her face, knocking her backward. Mia tried to twist aside, cried out in pain as his sword smacked across her back, sending her into the dust. The wooden sword crashed down beside her head as she rolled aside, slinging a handful of dirt. But the executus raised his shield with casual ease, countering with a vicious kick from that iron peg, right into her belly.

Mia doubled up and retched, blinded by the pain. Executus skewered the sand beside her head with his practice blade, looked down at her and growled.

"A thousand silver pieces? I'd not have paid a one."

Mia clawed her way to her knees, dusty hair stuck to the vomit on her chin. The other gladiatii dismissed her with sneers on their lips, returned to their training. Mia slung the shield off her arm, spat blood into the dust.

"Again," she demanded.

"No," Executus said. "I sought your measure. And now I have it in spades. Go wash off your defeat. The hour grows late. Your training begins amorrow."

Matteo walked forward slowly, helped Mia up from her knees. Standing with a wince, she stared across the dusty yard, rage burning inside her. She'd had a grip on the executus's footing, sure and true. A trick she'd performed countless times before—she should have bested him easily. But something . . . no, some*one*, had wrested control of the shadows, and saw her bested instead.

Furian looked up from beating the stuffing from his hapless training dummy, sweat gleaming on his beautiful face. Long dark hair blowing in the warm breeze. Silver torc glittering. Dark eyes fixed on hers.

"Bastard," she whispered.

The Unfallen returned to his training without another glance.

PRAYERS

"Well, this is going to be tricksy."

Mia took a long drag of her cigarillo, looking down on the pleasure house from their room in the taverna opposite. Jessamine stood at the window beside her, eyes narrowed as she watched the brothel door.

"You were expecting the leader of a braavi gang to just wander down the street with the map in her hand and fall onto your sword, Corvere?"

"You know I love your sarcasm more than anyone, Jess," Mia sighed. "But we've been cooped up in this room a week and I could use a change of tune."

"I know we've been up here a week, I'm the one who has to put up with your incessant fucking smoking."

". . . well, perhaps we could quarrel 'til the morrow and miss our opportunity entirely . . . ?"

Mia glanced to Mister Kindly, licking at his translucent paw on the bed.

"Your commentary is always appreciated."

". . . and freely given . . ."

"You're a little prick, you know that?"

". . . o, well and truly . . ."

Seven turns had passed since she'd arrived in the City of Bridges and Bones, and the only thing keeping Mia's belly from dissolving in a puddle of nerves were the passengers riding her shadow. Asking around her old haunts in Little Liis, Mia and Jessamine had tracked down their mark after a turn—the Toffs' headquarters was known to most of the lowlifes who peopled Little Liis. But finding their lair wasn't the problem. It was getting inside that was going to be the riddle.

The Toffs' stronghold was a well-appointed five-story palazzo named the Dog's Dinner. The bottom levels seemed a regular taverna, full of bawdy song and a crush of people. The third floor looked to be an ink den, and the top two, a brothel. Thugs *the size of small houses guarded the front doors, dressed up in expensive frock coats and powdered wigs that did little to hide the scars on their faces or the muscle beneath the fabric. Though no signage distinguished the building from its neighbors, this was braavi turf, and all the locals knew exactly what went on behind those doors.**

Their reconnaissance had gone flawlessly—being able to send two wisps of living darkness into the building to listen to every conversation and study every nook meant they knew everything that was set to happen this eve. But that didn't mean pulling this off was going to be easy.

Mia felt a tremble in her shadow, the kiss of a cool breeze. Eclipse coalesced from the darkness at her feet, shaking herself from head to tail.

"News?" Mia asked, cigarillo bobbing at her lips.

". . . SHE IS ON THE TOP FLOOR, CORNER OFFICE. SHE SPENT THE TURN ISSUING ORDERS, DRINKING, SMOKING, AND HAVING A GREAT DEAL OF SEX . . ."

"Fine work if you can get it," Jess said.

"The map is still being delivered here?" Mia asked.

". . . THE SELLER IS DUE TO ARRIVE SOMETIME WITHIN THE NEXT HOUR. THE EXCHANGE WILL TAKE PLACE IN THE DONA'S OFFICE . . ."

"So we have two options," Mia muttered. "We intercept the map before it arrives and end the Dona later, or wait for the seller and do them both at once."

". . . WE DO NOT KNOW WHAT THE SELLER LOOKS LIKE . . ."

"Presumably a dodgy bastard carrying a map case."

". . . you would still need to get into that office to end the dona regardless . . ."

"And therein lies the problem."

"You could steal inside?" Jessamine suggested. "Hidden in your shadows?"

Mia shook her head. "I can't see a thing under them. Groping around blind

---

*The braavi are a loose collective of gangs that run much of the criminal activity in Godsgrave—prostitution, larceny, and organized violence. Though a thorn in the side of Itreya's kings and Senate for centuries, the city's history is replete with bloody episodes where various city leaders tried (and failed) to dislodge them from their traditional roosts in Godsgrave's nethers.

It was Consul Julius Scaeva who first proposed the idea of paying the more powerful braavi an official stipend, and the first payment to them was made from his own personal fortune. Since then, the city has enjoyed a long tenure of peace and stability, and Scaeva a tremendous upswing in popularity.

As Mia so memorably stated in our first adventure, the so-called People's Senator is an unspeakable cunt, gentlefriends.

But he's not a stupid cunt.

inside a braavi den sounds a splendid way to get a sword in the tits. And the weaver did a particularly good job on these two. It'd be a shame to ruin them."

Jessamine squinted across the way.

"You could throw a grapple from this roof to the neighboring building. Jump the alley, get in through the Dinner's roof, work your way down."

"It's weeksend. Lots of people in the street. If one looks up . . ."

"Front door, then?"

Mia stared out across the street, muttering, "I'm terrible at the front door."

". . . you are getting better . . ."

"Liar."

". . . o, ye of little faith . . ."

"Faith never kept a drowning man from sinking." Mia dragged long on her cigarillo. "But admittedly, we don't have many options."

". . . we could stay up all nevernight and plait each other's hair and talk about boys . . . ?"

". . . MUST YOU ALWAYS PLAY THE FOOL, LITTLE MOGGY . . . ?"

". . . it is part of my charm . . ."

". . . THIS MUST BE SOME NEW DEFINITION OF CHARM WITH WHICH I AM UNAC-QUAINTED . . ."

"If you two are done," Mia growled, "go keep a lookout, aye?"

Emptiness filled her as her passengers departed, butterflies replacing them. Mia tried to shush her nerves, staring across at the braavi den and wondering what awaited her there. Close-quarter fighting. An inn full of hardened criminals. And whoever was selling the map would presumably bring muscle of their own. Bad odds.

Pushing aside her questions, Marius's warning ringing in her head, she crushed her cigarillo under heel.

"Right," she nodded. "I need a dress."

Mia walked across the crowded street as if she owned it, over the broken cobbles right toward the door of the Dog's Dinner.*

---

*A well-established taverna on Godsgrave's lower west side, which has undergone an astonishing number of name changes over the years. Originally called "the Burning Bush," its first owner was a retired brothel madam with a rather cheerful outlook on the ailments her many years in the saddle had given her. Purchased by a staunch monarchist years later, it was renamed "the Golden King" shortly before the overthrow of Francisco XV. After the good king's brutal murder, the pub was

Nevernight had fallen, wind howling down the thoroughfare. A summer storm had rolled in with it off the ocean, lukewarm rain coming down in thin curtains, the two suns hidden behind a mask of gray. But inclement weather was rarely a reason for folk in Godsgrave to stay inside on a weeksend, and the streets still bustled with folk on their way to their revels.

Little Liis was one of the more squalid sections of the 'Grave, but Liisian folk had flair, and growing up here as a girl, Mia had always found the colors and styles of their dress beautiful. They reminded her of her mother, truth told, and something in the music and aromas of this place called to the blood in her veins. Her outfit had been purloined from the chapel's wardrobe to fit in with the locals; leather britches and knee-length boots, a corset over a velvet shirt, a glittering necklet, all various shades of blood-red. If she got murdered in there, at least she'd leave a fine-looking corpse.

Up close, the doormen looked even more intimidating. They were under cover of the Dinner's front awning, but both still looked a little damp and more than a little surly. The gentle on the left was almost as wide as he was tall, and his comrade looked like he'd eaten his own parents for breakfast.

Wideboy held up a hand, stopping Mia short. "Hold there, Mi Dona."

"Merry nevernight, my lovely gentles," Mia smiled, dropped into a small curtsey.

"Can't come in 'ere," said Orphanboy, shaking his head.

"No riffraff," Wideboy agreed.

Mia looked down at her outfit, sounding mildly wounded. "Riffraff?"

Four drunken sailors who'd sit comfortably next to the definition of "riffraff" in Don Fiorlini's bestselling Itreyan Diction: the Definitive Guide *stepped up to the door.*

---

renamed "the Slaughtered Tyrant" in what most locals considered a fucking smart move.

Decades after, a slew of successive owners renamed the taverna "the Drunken Monk," "the Daughter's Bosom," the amusing if inexplicable "Seven Fat Bastards" (there were only two owners at the time, and neither was particularly obese). It was finally purchased by a braavi leader named Guiseppe Antolini and his new bride, Livia, and redubbed "the Lover's Vow."

Guiseppe disappeared soon after the pub's purchase, however, and Livia took over sole proprietorship of the hotel and leadership of the gang, renaming herself "the Dona" and the taverna "the Dog's Dinner." Rumor had it she'd discovered her beloved was diddling one of the serving girls, and according to the fireside gossip, she'd chopped off his wedding tackle and fed it to her dog, Oli.

Whether or not the rumor is true, it must be noted that the first sights to greet a newcomer to the establishment will be a well-fed pooch sitting by the hearth and a razor-sharp cleaver hanging over the bar.

"Good eve, gentlefriends," said Wideboy. "Welcome, welcome."

The man opened the doors, a burst of flute and laughter rang within, and the mariners stepped inside without a backward glance.

Mia smiled sweetly at Wideboy. "I've friends waiting insid—"

"Can't come in 'ere this eve," the big man said.

"Not serving your kind," Orphanboy nodded.

". . . My kind?"

The thugs grunted and nodded in unison.

"Let me understand this," Mia said. "You're a band of thieves, pimps, stand-over men and murderers. And you're telling me I'm *not* good enough to drink here?"

"Aye," said Wideboy.

"Fugoff," said his partner.

Mia adjusted her corset as meaningfully as possible. The braavi thugs stared at her without blinking. Finally, she folded her arms and sighed. "How much do you want?"

Orphanboy's eyes narrowed. "How much you got?"

"Two priests?"

The doorman looked up and down the street, then nodded. "Give it over, then."

Mia fished around her purse, and flipped one coin apiece to the doormen. The iron disappeared into their pockets quicker than a smokehound into the pipe on payday.

Mia stared at the pair, eyebrows rising. "Well?"

"Can't come in 'ere this eve," said Orphanboy.

"Not serving your kind," Wideboy agreed.

The pair stood aside for a second group of revelers (carrying a street sign and a somewhat troubled-looking sheep), bidding them good eve as they stepped inside. Every one of them was a man. Peering into the room beyond, Mia saw every single one of the clientele was also male. And somewhere in her head, Realization tipped its hat.

"Ohhhh," she said. "Riiiiight."

"Right," said Wideboy.

Orphanboy stroked his chin and nodded sagely.

"Well," she said.

". . . Well what?"

"Well, can I have my money back?" the girl asked.

"You're terrible at this," said Wideboy.

"Just awful," agreed Orphanboy.

Mia pouted. "Mister Kindly said I'm getting better."

"Whoever he is, Mister Kindly's a bloody liar."

The doormen folded their arms like a pair of synchronized dancers.

Mia sighed. "Merry nevernight, my lovely gentles."

And giving another bow, she marched back into the rain.

D on't you say a fucking word," she warned Mister Kindly.

She was crouched on a rooftop opposite the Dinner, staring out at a fourth-floor balcony. The not-cat sat beside her, tail swishing side to side.

". . . considering your childhood, it's little wonder you lack people skills . . ."

"Not. A. Fucking. Word."

". . . meow . . ."

". . . STRICTLY SPEAKING, THAT IS STILL A WORD . . . ," *Eclipse growled.*

"Aye." Mia held up a warning finger. "One more, and I officially enter your name in the Book of Grudges."

Mister Kindly lifted a translucent paw, placed it over the spot his mouth might've been. The rain was still spattering, warm and wet on her skin. Jessamine finished securing a length of silk line to an iron grapple, handed it dutifully to her Blade.

"Don't forget the map," the redhead warned. "And wait 'til I'm down on the street before you make your crossing. Nobody will look up if they're looking at me."

"I know. This was my idea, Jess."

"Were those britches your idea too?" Jessamine looked Mia up and down. "Because they're not doing that arse of yours any favors."

"O, stop, I fear my sides shall split."

"That's j—"

"Just what the britches said?" Mia rolled her eyes. "Aye, aye. Bravo, Mi Dona."

"I'll be waiting back here on the roof when you come out. And try not to get killed, neh?" Jess warned. "I'd be ever so disappointed I didn't do it myself."

Mia raised the knuckles. The redhead smirked, slipped down the stairwell without further insult. The crowd had thinned from the rain, but gentles were still spilling out of the Dinner, others staggering home after a merry nevernight. Mia watched Jessamine march across the street, straight for a young man just leaving the pleasure house.

"Youuuu bastard!" she cried, an accusing finger aimed at his face.

"Eh?" the young man blinked.

"You told me you were headed to your cousin's!" Jessamine shouted. "And here I find you, drinking and whoring behind my back!"

The gentle in question frowned in confusion. "Mi Dona, I ha—"

"Don't you 'Mi Dona' me!" Jessamine stepped closer, building up a head of steam. "Is this the example you wish to set for our son? O, Four blessed Daughters, why didn't I listen to Mother? She warned me about you!"

The revelers and braavi doormen watched as Jess launched into a scathing tirade, the fellow she was howling at barely able to get a word in edgewise. And with all eyes on the wronged paramour and her drunken beau, Mia took her chance.

Hurling her grapple across the fifteen-foot gap, she snagged it in the wrought-iron railing and tied it off tight. It was a four-story plunge to a sticky end on the cobbles below, and the railing was slick with rain. Yet, quick as silver, she stepped out into the void between buildings and began stealing across.

Fearless.

Reaching the rooftop of the bordello beside the Dinner, she peered over a chimney stack, not entirely surprised to find two miserable-looking braavi under a single umbrella, guarding the rooftop door. Mia was certain she could take the pair with the white wyrdglass in her pouch—hurling the arkemical globes at the men's feet would produce a cloud of Swoon big enough to knock both unconscious. But wyrdglass made a noteworthy bang when it popped, and the noise might raise an alarm.

". . . mpphgglmm . . . ," said Mister Kindly.

"What?"

". . . HE SAID MPPHGGLMM . . ."

"Daughters, all right, all right, you can speak."

The not-cat cleared its throat.

". . . which room is the dona's . . . ?"

Eclipse nodded to the corner windows on the top floor. The curtains were drawn, no sign of what might be going on inside.

". . . SHE HAD FIVE MEN IN THERE WITH HER, WHEN LAST I LOOKED . . ."

"I don't like the idea of bursting in blind," Mia muttered. "And the map might not be here yet."

". . . start in the ink den, work your way up, hide until it arrives . . . ?"

"That sounds suspiciously like a plan."

Mia dropped onto a narrow ledge on the bordello's third floor, and leapt across the rain-soaked gap to the balcony on the Dinner. Waiting a moment to listen for any commotion, she peered through the keyhole to the bedchamber beyond. Four figures in various stages of undress were passed out in a tangle of limbs on a four-poster bed, empty ink needles on the furs beside them. Dead to the world.

Quiet as shadows, Mia retrieved her lockpicks from her boot heel, sweet-talked the balcony door and slipped inside. The quartet didn't stir from their inkdreams.

She shook off the rain and was sneaking past the bed when a soft knock sounded. Mia was across the room in a flash, hiding behind the door as it opened gently.

"Service?" a young voice said. "Mi Dons? I have your sugarwater."

A girl stepped inside, a golden courtesan's masque on her face. She looked barely a teenager, but dressed as a woman—crushed black taffeta and cheap chiffon. She carried a silvered tray, four fine goblets and a decanter of sea-blue liquid. Lowering her voice as she saw the slumbering inkfiends on the bed, she turned to push the door closed and silence the celebrations downstairs.

Lightning flashed across the skies outside. A hand reached from behind her, holding her tray. Another about her mouth.

"Hush now," Mia whispered.

The lass stood still as a statue in Tyrant's Row.

"I mean no harm, love," Mia said. "You've my word. I'll take my hand away if you promise not to cry out?"

The girl nodded, chest heaving. Mia edged her hand from the girl's lips, stepped back, hand on her gravebone sword. The girl turned slowly, looked her up and down—the blades, the black, the stare—her breath coming even quicker as she realized what Mia was about. Glancing toward the bed, looking for marks of murder.

"I'm not here for them," Mia promised.

"Are you . . . here for me?"

Mia looked her over—the low neckline, the tightly cinched corsetry, the golden masque. A woman twice her age might find herself comfortable in such an outfit. Might revel in the power it gave. But this one was barely more than a child.

. . . Barely more than a child?

Daughters, what am I?

She should be away about her business, she knew it. The Dona was upstairs, the map was on its way, and Mia needed to end one and steal the other by the morrow. But there was something about this girl. Just one of dozens working inside these walls. Could she have ended in a place like this if Mercurio hadn't found her? If her life had been just a little different?

This was softness, she knew it. She should be steel. But still . . .

"How old are you?" she found herself asking.

"Fourteen," the girl replied.

Mia shook her head. "Is this what you want?"

A blink. "What?"

"Is this what you dreamed of being?" Mia asked. "When you were younger?"

"I . . ." The girl's eyes were locked on the sword at Mia's belt. Her voice turned cold with self-mockery. "I used to pray Aa would make me a princess."

Mia smiled. "None of us get to be princesses, love."

"No," the girl said simply. "No, we don't."

Silence hung in the room like morning fog. Mia only stared, as she often did, letting the quiet ask her questions for her.

"Horses," the girl finally said, tugging her dress higher. "I used to dream of working with horses. A little merchant's wagon, perhaps. Something simple."

"That sounds nice."

"I'd have a black stallion named Onyx," the girl said. "And a white mare named Pearl. And we'd ride wherever the wind blew, nobody to stop us."

"So why don't you do that?"

The lass looked around the room, the bordello beyond it. The light dying in her eyes as she shrugged helplessly. "No choice."

"You could choose the purses at their waists." Mia pointed at the trio of marrowborn on the four-poster. "The jewels at their throats. I know a man called Mercurio who lives in the necropolis. If you told him Mia sent you, he could help set you up. Someplace with horses, maybe. Someplace you want to be."

A glance upstairs. Fear in shadowed eyes. "They'd catch me."

"Not if you're quick. Not if you're clever."

Thunder rolled beyond the window.

"I'm not," the girl said.

"That's Fear talking. Never listen to him. Fear is a coward."

The girl looked Mia up and down, shaking her head. "I'm not like you."

Mia could see her reflection in the serving girl's stare as lightning arced across the skies outside. Death pale skin. Gravebone at her side. Shadows in her eyes.

"I'm not sure you want to be like me," she said. "I just doubt this"—she reached out and untied the golden masque—"is anything like you."

The face behind the gold was thin. An old bruise at her lip. Tired, pretty eyes.

"But it's your choice. Always yours."

The girl looked to the inkfiends. Back to Mia's eyes.

"Are there many of them upstairs?" Mia asked.

The girl nodded. Licked the bruise at her mouth. "The worst of them."

"There's a package being delivered here this eve. Do you know anything of it?" The girl shook her head. "They don't tell me much."

Mia looked down at the crystalware goblets, the decanter and the silver tray. Up at the girl and her tired eyes. The girl was staring at a purse among the inkfiend's scattered clothes. A golden ring on another's finger.

"What's your name?" Mia asked.

The girl blinked. Looked back at Mia. "Belle."

"Could you do me a favor, Belle?"

Sudden wariness dawned in the girl's eyes. "What kind of favor?"
Mia walked a slow circle around her. Nodded once.
"Can I borrow that dress?"

Mia and Matteo were escorted from their sparring session by two guards wearing tabards of the Familia Remus. Staring at that falcon sigil on their chests, Mia felt that sinking feeling in her belly growing worse. Sidonius limped out from an infirmary at the keep's rear. The big man's nose had been set with a wooden splint after Mia's beating, fresh stitches at his brow. The girl called Maggot followed him, wandering over to the big mastiff and letting him lick the man's blood from her fingers. She looked at Mia, again gifting her that small, shy smile.

Not knowing quite what to make of the girl, and despite the bitter sting of her defeat at the hands of the executus, Mia smiled back.

The guards collected Sidonius, and the new recruits were marched up to the great double doors at the keep's rear. There, they were met by a slender woman with long gray hair and three circles branded into her cheek. She was in her late forties, and carried herself with an almost regal air. A flowing dress of fine red silk hugged her body, and her neck was encircled with a silver torc, similar to Furian's.

"I am Anthea, majordomo of this house," she said. "I manage the domina's affairs in these walls. You will refer to me as Magistrae. You are to be bathed and fed before being locked down for the nevernight. If you have questions, you may speak."

Sidonius rubbed a hand across his bloody chin, looked the woman up and down.

"Will you wash my back for me, Dona?"

The magistrae glanced at the guards. The men drew wooden truncheons and proceeded to beat the bleeding shit out of Sidonius right there in the foyer. Mia rolled her eyes, wondering how the Itreyan could be so dense. After a hard drubbing—his second of the turn—Sidonius lay on the tiled floor in a spatter of his own blood.

"That's a n-no . . . I take it . . . ?"

"Mistake me not for some simple servant, cur," Magistrae said, her dark eyes roaming the COWARD burned into his chest. "I have known our domina since she was a child, and when she is absent, I am her voice in this house. Now cease your bleeding upon my tiles and follow."

Sidonius wobbled to his feet, brow and lips dripping red. Mia watched the magistrae from the corner of her eye. The woman reminded her of her father's majordomo—a Liisian named Andriano—who was head of this household back when the Corvere colors still flew upon the walls. He too lived in bondage, but carried himself like a freeman. Anthea seemed cut from the same cloth.

The more things change . . .

"May I ask a question, Magistrae?" Mia asked.

Anthea looked her over with a careful eye before replying. "Speak."

"I see falcons hanging on the courtyard walls." Mia winced, massaging her bruised ribs. "But is our domina not of the Familia Leonides?"

"The falcon is the sigil of Marcus Remus," the woman nodded. "Aa bless and keep him. This was his house, awarded for his service to the Republic after the Kingmaker Rebellion. Now he is gone to his eternal rest by the Hearth, the estate passes to his widow, your new domina."

The sinking feeling in Mia's belly reached all the way down to her toes.

I fucking knew it . . .

Mia had no idea where he might be, but she could almost hear Mister Kindly's rebuke in her ears. She hadn't just failed to win a place with the collegium she'd intended, she'd also fallen into servitude to the wife of the justicus she'd *murdered*? Her scheme was drifting farther down the sewer with every passing turn . . .

Be still. Be patient. Leona will never know.

Mia bowed her head, followed the magistrae obediently. They were escorted through a broad hall at the keep's rear, the trio all limping after their beatings. Mia was reeling from the news about Leona, about the presence of another darkin, but somewhere in the back of her mind, the child who'd walked these halls was struck by how much Crow's Nest had changed. The layout was untouched, but the decor . . .

Dona Corvere had favored an opulent look, but now the halls were plain—the beautiful tapestries and carpets replaced by suits of armor and weapons of war. Mia wanted to see her old room, the view of the ocean from the balconies, but she and her fellows were led down a winding stair to an antechamber outside the cellar. An iron portcullis blocked them from going any farther, a complex mekwerk device on the wall beside it. A guard inserted an odd key, worked a series of levers. The portcullis rose, and Magistrae ushered Mia and the others inside.

Darius Corvere had used the vast sublevel as a living area for the brutal summer months, but Mia could see it had been refitted as a barracks. The space had been partitioned into six-by-six cells, lined with long rows of heavy iron bars.

Very generous of the dona to let her pets live underground . . .

Walking past the cages, Mia noted the fresh straw, the thick chains. Arkemical globes glowed on the wall. The barracks smelled of sweat and shit, but at least they were cool. The guards kept them moving, marching to the end of a long corridor, where they found a large bathhouse, hung thick with steam. Mia and her fellows were ushered in by Magistrae, the guards left outside. The older woman looked at them expectantly.

"Off with your clothes," she ordered.

Another girl her age might have blushed. Trembled or simply refused. But Mia saw her body as just another weapon, as dangerous as any blade. Weaver Marielle had gifted her curves sharp enough to almost kill a man if she wished it, and Mia had murdered more men than she could rightly count.

What matter now to show a little skin?

And so, she stripped off her rags and boots without hesitation, stood naked in the steam. Sidonius was still too shaky from his beating to take much notice, but she saw Matteo drinking in her body from the corner of his eyes. Magistrae pointed to a stone bench near the pool. Mia saw razors, combs, a bevy of soaps.

"Gladiatii bathe together, eat together, fight together," the woman explained. "But until you survive the Winnowing, you will tend to your own ablutions. Mark me well; I'll not tolerate filth beneath this roof. And have a care with that hair of yours, girl." Magistrae looked at Mia's long, dirty locks. "If I find a single flea in it, I'll have the lot chopped off."

The woman raised one gray, sculpted eyebrow, inviting questions. After a moment's silence, she nodded curtly.

"I will return in twenty minutes. Keep me waiting, taste the lash as your reward."

Magistrae stalked away, the guards remaining stationed outside the door. Mia waded into the bath, sinking down with a long sigh. The temperature was glorious, and she luxuriated in the sensation, running her hands over her skin. Pushing back her hair, she finally surfaced, blinking the water from her lashes. She fixed Matteo in her stare, let herself rise in the water just enough that her breasts showed above the surface. The boy had his hands at his crotch, unsuccessfully trying to cover his growing erection as he stepped into the bath.

"Four Daughters, you'll have someone's eye out with that," Sidonious growled. "Anyone'd think you'd never seen a pair of baps before."

Matteo raised the knuckles and Mia found herself laughing. She reached for a cake of honeysoap, wondering how a peace offering might fare. Thugs often stood down once you stood up to their bullshit . . .

"If you weren't such a pig, I'd find you more amusing, Sidonius."

"Aye, well, if you weren't such a cunt, I'd find you more attractive, little Crow."

"I think I'll learn to live with the heartache."

The Itreyan smirked, gingerly touched his broken nose. Though she'd given him a drubbing, he seemed not to take it personally, and Mia decided Sidonius was one of those fellows who worked out his feelings through the application of violence. The kind who'll walk into a taverna and beat the wailing shit out of the first man to look at him crossways, but the moment the fight is done, will be calling his foe "brother" and buying him drinks. Now that she'd given him a walloping, he seemed more kindly disposed. Though watching Sidonius prod his new sutures, she still wouldn't be willing to bet whether he'd rather fuck or murder her.

"Who stitched you?" she asked, blinking suds from her eyes. "That young girl?"

"Aye," Sidonius nodded. "Maggot they call her."

"What kind of name is that?"

The big man sank up to his chin in the water. "No clue. But she's swift with a needle. Good thing, too. She'll have more stitching to do after the Winnowing."

Matteo finally dragged his eyes away from Mia's breasts, frowning.

"What is this Winnowing they speak of?"

Sidonius scoffed. "Where you from, boy?"

"Ysiir. Down near Dust Falls."

"They got no arenas down there?"

Matteo shook his head. "I'd never seen the ocean until a month ago. Never even left my village. And now I'm here. Locked up with Itreyan pigs and Dweymeri brutes."

"Watch your mouth." Sidonius raised an eyebrow. "I'm Itreyan."

"Aye," Mia said. "And the most brilliant boy I ever met was Dweymeri."

Sidonius nodded. "I'd leave that shit in the sewer if I was you, country-boy."

Matteo mumbled apology, fell silent. Minutes passed, the boy fumbling with the soap, finally dropping the cake and fishing about for it in the water.

"How'd you end up here?" Mia asked.

The boy shrugged, steam sticking those dark curls to his skin. "My da sold me. Gambling debts. Foisted me off for want of coin."

"Aa's cock," Sidonius growled. "And I thought *I* was cold-blooded."

"You're half-decent with a blade," Mia said. "Where'd you learn to fight?"

"My uncle." Matteo ran a hand through his hair, Mia idly watching the muscles at play in his arm as she combed her knots. "I was going to join the legion. I hoped I might get posted to a big city one turn. I always wanted to see the City of Bridges and Bones."

"Perhaps you will," Mia said. "They hold the *Venatus Magni* in Godsgrave."

"What's that?"

"The greatest games in the calendar," Sidonius replied. "Held at truelight, when all of Aa's eyes are open in the sky. The purses are fortunes to the sanguila who win them. And to the gladiatii who wins the *magni*? He knows greatest prize of all."

Hope gleamed in Matteo's deep brown eyes. "Freedom?"

The big Itreyan nodded. "A gladiatii can buy his way free if he wins enough coin. But the gladiatii who wins the *magni* has freedom handed to him by god himself."

The boy frowned in confusion, obviously oblivious. Sidonius rolled his eyes.

"You heard the tale of the beggar and the slave?"*

"Aye."

---

* A parable from the Gospels of Aa. In his wisdom, one fine weeksend, the Light God sought to test the worthiness of his subjects. And so, dressed as a beggar, he sat outside the grand temple to his name, dressed in rags with an alms bowl before him.

The king walked by in his golden crown, and the beggar pleaded for a coin. But the king told him nay.

The cardinal strode past in his silken robe, and the beggar pleaded again. But the cardinal gave him none.

Then a slave came by, and in his wisdom, Aa asked nothing, for the man had naught to give. But seeing the beggar's plight, the slave took his cloak—his only possession in the world—and wrapped it around the old beggar's shoulders. And Aa threw off his guise and stood, and the slave fell to his knees, amazed.

"Stand, I pray thee," said almighty Aa. "For even in thy poverty, thou hast dignity. And I say thou shalt kneel to no man again."

And the Light God granted the slave his freedom. And the slave was mighty pleased. And nobody stopped to ask what the slave was planning to give the *next* beggar he found if the first one hadn't been a god, or how it's not really sound economic policy for kings to wander about giving taxpayer money to the destitute when public infrastructure is in such dire need of overhaul, or why the creator of the universe had nothing better to do on a weeksend afternoon than come down to earth to fuck with people.

Pfft.

Parables.

"Well, to honor the God of Light during truelight, every beggar in the 'Grave is fed from the Republic's coffers. And the winner of the *magni* is given his freedom by the grand cardinal himself. Clad in naught but rags, just like Aa was in the gospel."

Sidonius leaned forward, eyes glittering.

"And then, if that weren't enough, the bloody *consul* hands you your victor's laurel. Imagine it. Crowd going berserk. That god-bothering bastard Duomo dressed like a beggar, and that marrowborn wanker Scaeva kissing your arse in front of the entire arena." Sidonius grinned like a madman. "Every woman in the 'Grave would know your name. You'd be swimming in cunny for the rest of your life, countryboy."

Mia looked to the ripples on the water before her. Imagining it, just as she'd imagined it for months now. Grand Cardinal Duomo, standing within arm's reach, dressed in nothing but his beggar's robes.

No cathedral around him.

No holy vestments around his shoulders.

And no trinity hanging around his neck . . .

And beside him, Consul Scaeva, victor's laurel waiting in his hand . . .

"And all I need do is win the *magni*?" Matteo asked.

Sidonius guffawed. "All? Aye, that's *all* you have to do. Just win the greatest games in the Republic. Against the finest gladiatii under the suns. This collegium hasn't even *won a berth* in the great games yet."

"Well, how do we do that?"

"With difficulty," Mia sighed. "A collegium that earns enough laurels leading up to truelight can send gladiatii. But apparently this is our domina's first competitive season, and it seems she's but one victor's laurel to her name." Mia scowled. "Furian's."

"And we three are a long way from the sands just yet," Sidonius growled. "Before we're even counted among the gladiatii, we must survive the Winnowing."

"So come to explanation, then," Matteo demanded. "What *is* this Winnowing?"

"A cull," Sidonius said. "They hold them before every major games in the lead-up to the *magni*. Separate the wheat from the chaff."

"Nobody knows what shape the Winnowings take," Mia explained. "The editorii change the format each time. But the next one is in two weeks. At Blackbridge."

Matteo swallowed thickly, muscle in his jaw twitching.

"But if we don't know what the format will be, how do we prepare for it?"

"Do you pray?" Mia asked.

". . . Aye."

Mia shrugged.

"I'd start there if I were you."

CHAPTER 9

STEPPING

Mia walked slowly, service tray balanced on her upturned palms. Other girls passed her in the hallway, carrying drinks or bowls of purple slumberbloom or phials of ink. Her shirt had been left behind in her room, but she still wore her britches beneath the corset and gown, sword and stiletto and a pouch of wyrdglass strapped to her thighs. She proceeded up the hallway carefully, hoping she portrayed an image of poise, rather than that of a girl with a small armory bumping against her nethers.

She reached the stairs at the end of the hall, made to breeze past the two lumps of muscle there without a word. One spoke as she passed, freezing her in her tracks.

"Good eve, Belle."

She'd tied the golden courtesan masque over her own, propped Belle's powdered wig atop her head. She was a good inch or two taller than the serving girl, and harder muscled, but her curves were around the same, and that was where the bruiser was spending most of his eye time.

"Lazlo," she said, giving a small curtsey.

"A stupid one," Belle had told her. "Just give him a flirt and he'll let you past."

"You're looking dashing as ever," Mia smiled.

"Where you goin' with that?" the second man asked, eying the tray.

"Dario," Belle had warned. "A mean one. But even stupider than Lazlo."

Mia nodded upstairs. "Toliver and Vespa ordered a bottle for the Dona."

Dario looked to Lazlo, muttering. "We're not supposed to let anyone up 'til—"

"Aa's cock, man, leave her to it," Lazlo said. He trailed one finger gently down Mia's arm, and the girl had to steel herself from taking his hand off at the shoulder. "You head on upstairs, little dove."

Skin crawling at the thought of a grown man calling a fourteen-year-old his "little dove," Mia trod carefully up the stairs. From what Dario had said, the map still wasn't here yet, but the seller had to be arriving soon. She could hear rain on the roof now, walking down a polished hallway hung with nudes of beautiful men and women. A double door flanked by two guards waited for her at the corridor's end, and thanks to Eclipse's scouting, she knew the Dona's office was beyond it.

"... FIVE MEN AND YOUR MARK INSIDE ...," *came a soft growl at her feet.*

"... though one of them will prove little trouble ..."

Four men, plus the Dona, plus whoever the map dealer brought with them.

Black Mother, they don't make it easy, do they?

Mia had thought perhaps to wait in a side room until she heard the seller arrive, but the guards on the office door were staring right at her.

"Eclipse," she whispered. "Head downstairs and look for our seller."

Feeling her shadow ripple, she adjusted her wig and walked blithely up to the office, greeted both men with a smile.

"Maxis, Donato, pleasant eve," she said, curtseying.

"Belle, you shouldn't b—"

Before Donato could finish his objection, Mia rapped on the door with her foot. After a moment, it swung wide, and she looked up into the face of a tall Dweymeri man, his features inked with artful tattoos, his broad chest wrapped in a fine waistcoat with gold buttons. He scowled at the pair of guards beside the door.

"Thought I said no visitors 'til she arrives."

"I tried to stop 'er, blame fucking Laz—"

"Who is it?" called a low, musical voice from inside.

With one last black scowl at the guards, the Dweymeri replied over his shoulder.

"Belle. And booze."

"Four Daughters, send her in. I could drink the Sea of Stars."

The braavi thug stared at Mia a moment longer, then stepped aside.

Mia breezed past,* noting the rapier and stiletto sheathed at the thug's belt. The room beyond was a grand boudoir, three other braavi thugs waiting around the periphery. Though all were dressed like marrowborn dandies, each carried a small armory. Fine art hung on the walls and red silk was draped on every surface. A large bed dominated the setting, and a pretty young man lay sleeping upon it.

"Set it over there, Belle. And be quick about it, there's a love."

A figure in the shadows spoke, a low and dusky voice Mia finally identified as

---

* Well, as breezy as one can get with a gravebone longsword and a bag of arkemical explosives pressed against one's crotch.

female. As the speaker stepped into the light, Mia saw dark hair, dagger-sharp cheekbones. She wore a monocle on a silver chain about her neck, and was slipping a fine-cut silk shirt over her head. Mia recognized her from the sketch in Solis's scroll case immediately—the Dona, leader of the Toffs.

"Don't mind him, he's down for a while." The Dona smiled, nodding to the snoozing figure on the bed. "Lads today. No stamina at all."

Mia offered what she hoped was a polite laugh, set the tray down where she was bid. The guards were barely paying attention to her—two were close enough to get caught in a wyrdglass blast, and her shadow could hold at least one other in place. The sweetboy on the bed would be no drama. Five short steps and she could have the Dona's throat open. It would all depend on who the map seller brought wi—

"... SHE COMES ...," came a whisper in her ear.

"Dona," called one of the door guards. "Company."

The braavi leader nodded, motioning Mia toward the corner.

"Plant yourself over there and look mysterious, love. But plants don't talk, aye?"

Mia nodded, slinking back into the shadows. She heard brief murmurs at the boudoir door, thunder cracking outside the window. A figure walked past the guards—short, decidedly feminine—clad in a loose outfit of mortar gray, slightly damp from the storm outside. Her face was cowled, covered, a pair of sparkling blue eyes visible between the folds. An assortment of blades was strapped to her body, and Mia's heart beat quicker as she spied a wooden map case slung over her shoulder.

"Well, well," the figure said. "This is nice and dramatic, isn't it?"

"You came alone," the Dona mused.

"That's the way I work," the newcomer replied, strolling into the room. Her words were muffled under her cowl, but there was something ...

Those eyes.

That voice ...

It couldn't be ...

The newcomer glanced at the naked young man on the bed, Mia with her too-tight corset. "Nice view. But it's a touch crowded, don't you think?"

"That's the way I work," the Dona replied. "And I've two golden rules in this life, little one—never trust a man who speaks of his mother without kindness, and never trust a woman who wears a masque without cause."

The newcomer rolled her eyes, but nevertheless pulled her cowl down, releasing long warbraids of golden blond. And as Mia's belly flipped sideways and all the way around, the newcomer pulled away the fabric, revealing a face Mia knew almost as well as her own.

Lightning crashed, Mia's fingernails biting her palm.

Black fucking Mother . . .

It was Ashlinn Järnheim.

When last they'd seen each other, they'd been facing down across a dusty thoroughfare in Last Hope. The Luminatii invasion had failed, the justicus was slain. But a trinity around Ashlinn's neck had held Mia at bay long enough for Ash to escape.

And now she was here in Godsgrave.

Carrying the very item Mia had been sent to steal . . .

What the 'byss is going on here?

"You have the map?" the Dona asked.

"You have the money?" Ashlinn replied.

The Dona nodded to a guard, who tossed a clinking pouch in the girl's direction. Ashlinn snatched it from the air, opened the drawstring and took out a single coin. Not a copper beggar, not an iron priest, but . . .

Gold.

Mia shook her head.

Goddess, a fortune . . .

"Now," the Dona said. "Your half of the bargain, if it please you."

Ashlinn slung the map case off her shoulder, tossed it to the Dona. The woman opened one end with a soft click, pulling a rolled piece of vellum a little ways out of the case. Mia caught a glimpse of strange writing, a sickle-shaped symbol in the corner.

"Well," Ashlinn sighed. "Pleasant as this is, I spied a pretty redhead downstairs so I'll just be . . ."

Ashlinn's sentence trailed off as the guards at the entrance pushed the door closed with all due drama. Mia shook her head, calculating whether she should reach for her wyrdglass or longsword first. Deciding on the arkemy, she cursed Ashlinn for a fool—marching into a braavi den and mouthing off like she owned it. Did she honestly think this was going to end another way?

The fool in question glanced over her shoulder, blue eyes narrowed.

"Could you ask your fancylads to step out of my way, please, Dona?"

"I'm afraid not," the braavi leader replied. "The grand cardinal was rather specific about what we were to do with you after coin changed hands."

Mia's heart surged at the Dona's words.

Cardinal Duomo? How is he mixed up in all this?

Thunder crashed outside the window again, lighting flickering through the curtain cracks. The Dona leaned against her desk and smiled.

"I confess, I'm surprised you made this so easy, little one. Duomo warned me you and your father were as sharp as razors."

"I'd heard the same about you," Ashlinn said, eyes on the braavi thugs now slowly fanning out around her. *"Imagine my disappointment."*

"Fear not, it shan't last long," the Dona smiled.

Ashlinn nodded to the map case in the Dona's hands.

"Do you even know where that leads?"

"No. I don't stick my nose into what doesn't concern me."

"You might want to work on that," Ashlinn smiled. *"Because a nosy person might have spied the false bottom in the case they'd been handed. And a person not so fond of her own voice might have heard the flint that sparked the fuse on the tombstone bomb inside."*

The Dona's eyes widened. Ashlinn threw herself aside, Mia barely having the presence of mind to hurl herself behind the bed before the map case exploded with an earsplitting boom. The Dona was blasted across the room, dead before she hit the floor. Three guards were caught in the arkemical fireball, the Dweymeri smashed through the doors, his waistcoat aflame, the other thugs tossed about like burning straw.

The room was filled with choking smoke, Mia's skull pounding from the blast.

"Maw's teeth," she spat, trying to rise.

"... MIA ...!"

"... are you well ...?"

Ashlinn uncovered her ears, picked herself off the ground. She snatched up her sack of gold, and drawing a short blade from her belt, plunged it into the braavi groaning on the floor beside her. Satisfied that the Dona was already dead, she quickly perished any guard who was still moving, then turned toward the serving girl in her smoking chiffon lying beside the bed.

"Apologies, Mi Dona, but I ..."

Mia rolled over onto her back. Her masque had been knocked clear in the blast, her ears ringing, her vision blurred. Mister Kindly coalesced on her shoulder, Eclipse at her feet, translucent fangs bared in a snarl that could be felt through the floor.

"'Byss and blood," Ashlinn breathed.

Eyes as blue as empty skies were fixed on the shadowcat on Mia's shoulder. Focusing now on his mistress herself.

"... Mia?"

"Four fucking Daughters ...," came another voice.

Mia squinted through the haze, saw Lazlo, Dario and three other Toffs at the office door, staring in horror at the carnage beyond. Dario clapped eyes on the corpse of their leader. Lazlo, the figure swathed in gray.

"*Kill 'er!*" one of the thugs roared.

Without a word, Ashlinn was dashing toward the window, hurling a dagger and shattering the glass. The Toffs charged in a mob, and more out of instinct than forethought, Mia reached under her dress and threw one of her white wyrdglass globes at their feet. The arkemical sphere burst with a loud bang, a cloud of thick white Swoon engulfing the thugs.

Ashlinn climbed through the window, grabbed a silk line tied to a stone gargoyle above. Without a backward glance, she was up the wall and gone.

Mia staggered to her feet, head still ringing, swaying to the windowsill. She was in a tight corset and long gown; not the easiest gear to be scaling brothel walls in, even without a concussion. But, fearless as ever, she seized hold of the line and swung out over the five-story drop, scrambling onto the roof just in time to see Ashlinn leap across to the bordello next door.

"*Eclipse, go get Jessamine!*" *she barked.* "*Mister Kindly, with me!*"

The shadowwolf disappeared, Mister Kindly flitted across the roof after their quarry. Shaking her head to clear the ringing, Mia followed hard. Truth was, her boots weren't made for a chase scene, and the rain had made the roof tiles as treacherous as the snake she was chasing. As Ashlinn dropped off the bordello roof, Mia skidded to a cursing halt, hacking at her skirts with her gravebone stiletto so she could run faster.

Mia's mind was reeling. It'd been eight months since she'd laid eyes on Ashlinn Järnheim, and she could scarce believe the girl was here now. She and her father had been in alliance with Justicus Remus to bring down the Red Church. Now she was in league with the grand cardinal?

Mia pushed the questions from her mind, tore away the rest of her sodden skirts and ran on. Peering over the bordello roof, she saw Ashlinn dropping to the cobbles below, too far away to reach her shadow. Fearless of the fall, she flipped over the edge, scaling from window to window, fingers white on the rain-slick stone. Reaching the cobbles, she dashed off through the Godsgrave streets, and over the Bridge of Tears.*

Ashlinn ran like the Mother herself was on her tail, weaving in and out of the

---

* Situated near the bordellos and pleasure houses of Little Liis, the Bridge of Tears is supposedly named for the sorrows of a thousand jilted lovers, who over the years have stood upon the bridge and wept upon discovery their beloved had sought the company of a sweetboy or sugargirl in the brothel district.

In truth, the bridge earned its moniker long before the surrounding borough became a den of iniquity, and is actually named for the tear-shaped stonework supporting its main arch.

Still, never let the truth get in the way of a good yarn, gentlefriends.

crowd like smoke. Mia sprinted in pursuit, losing sight of her at least twice, turned aside in the maze of canals and dogleg alleys. But Mister Kindly flitted from rooftop to rooftop, leaping across awning and gable like the wind and calling above the summer storm.

". . . left, left . . ."

". . . alley beside the chandlers . . ."

". . . no, your other left . . ."

Mia broke out onto a main drag, sliding beneath the axle of a galloping horse and cart and skirting the handfuls of limping jacks Ashlinn was throwing behind her.* Row after row of houses, temples with windows like empty eyes, thin bridges and winding canals. They were headed toward Godsgrave's marrowborn district now, the Ribs rising into the storm-washed skies. Ashlinn dashed down a dead-end alley, kicked left then right up the stonework, scrabbling over the broken glass at the top.

Mia followed, cutting her palms bloody. Ash was running across the rooftops again now, the terra-cotta treacherous with the rain. Leaping over the gap between one roof and another, Mia almost slipped as a tile cracked beneath her sodden boots. If she fell, it'd be a broken leg at best, a shattered spine at worst.

Where the fuck are Eclipse and Jessamine?

Mia saw the Basilica Grande looming ahead—a gothic masterpiece of marble spires and stained glass. The trinity of three suns glittered in every window, gleamed atop every steeple. Mia couldn't help but recall the truedark when she was fourteen—the dozens of men she'd murdered here in her failed attempt to kill Consul Scaeva. Ash knew Mia's weakness for the Everseeing's holy symbols— she was obviously hoping the basilica grounds were hallowed enough to repel the darkin on her heels.

Clever girl. But it doesn't work that way . . .

Ash reached to her belt, gathered another thin line and grapple. Throwing it across to the basilica's gutters, Ash swung across the gap and scrambled onto the roof. Mia ran harder, hoping to leap the distance, but even with Mister Kindly eating her fear, she knew the gap was too wide. Skidding to a halt at the edge, she watched Ashlinn clamber up the tiles. Gasping for breath. Heart hammering in her chest.

Mia drew a throwing knife from her boot, took aim. She'd poisoned her blades with Swoon, and even a scratch would be enough to drop the girl like a bag of bricks. But, much as she wanted to, Mia realized . . .

---

* Limping jacks: Godsgrave streetslang for caltrops, so named because of their similarity to jumping jacks, and the fact that people who decide to run through clusters of them tend to end up . . . O, you get the gist.

I need her alive.

She lowered the blade, looked to the cobblestones thirty feet below. A novice wandering the cathedral grounds looked up and saw her, jaw dropping in surprise.

"Shit . . . ," she breathed.

". . . a distance like that should not trouble you . . ."

Mia looked to the shadowcat at her feet. Down to the gap again.

"I can't jump that far, it's impossible."

". . . not so long ago, you stepped from the top of the philosopher's stone all the way to the isle of godsgrave to this very cathedral. skipping across the city like a child over puddles . . ."

"That was during truedark, Mister Kindly."

". . . you did so again in the quiet mountain . . ."

"Aye, and the suns have never seen inside that place."

". . . it is raining. aa's eyes are hidden behind the clouds . . ."

"I'm not strong enough out here, don't you see?"

The not-cat sighed, shaking his head.

Ashlinn had reached the apex of the cathedral's roof, turning to look at Mia. Her blond hair had grown longer, damp with rain and plastered to her tanned skin. Her pretty eyes were the blue of sunburned skies. Mia felt her fingers curl to fists, remembering what she'd done to Tric.

Ashlinn smiled. Holding two fingers to her eyes, pointing at Mia across the gap and speaking in the wordless sign language of Tongueless.

I see you.

And with a small smile, the Vaanian girl blew Mia a kiss.

Rage came then. Watching Ash scuttle away toward the basilica's bell tower. Mister Kindly could still follow; Mia could scramble down to street level and give chase. But the lead Ash now had was a long one, and truth was, all the cigarillos she'd been smoking lately weren't doing Mia's constitution any favors.

She was sick of running.

All right, fuck it then . . .

Mia reached out across the gulf, beneath that muddy gray sky. The shadows were indistinct with the sunlight veiled, but she could still sense two of Aa's eyes, burning in the heavens. A thin film of cloud and rain wasn't enough to rein in the rage of a god, and Mia could feel it scorching the back of her neck. But still . . .

But still . . .

She knew the dark. Knew its song. Remembering the way she'd felt it at true-dark. Seeped into the cracks of this city's pores, puddling in the catacombs under its skin. The dark she cast at her feet, the dark that lived inside her chest, her womb, all the places the light had never touched. And teeth gritted, trembling, she reached into those warm and hollow places, stretched out her hand to the shadow of the bell tower

and Stepped

across

the hollow space

between.

Mia reeled, vertigo swelling in her belly, vomit in her throat. Swaying backward, she tottered as all the world shifted beneath her, almost toppling to her death on the wrought-iron fence below. She realized she was on the basilica roof, rain slicking the shingles beneath her feet, blinking hard and trying to regain her balance as Ashlinn loomed out of the blinding light, dagger in hand.

"... mia ... !"

She barely dodged, bending backward as the blade sliced the air. Mia raised her gravebone sword, trying to regain her footing. Bile in her mouth. Sweat in her eyes.

"... mia ... !"

Ash struck again, forcing Mia's back against the bell tower's wall. Mia raised her longsword into guard, gasping and blinking and trying to stop the world from spinning.

"Learned a few new tricks, love?" Ashlinn smiled, dagger in hand.

The girl reached down her leg, fishing about inside her boot. It took her a moment, but finally she found what she sought, drawing out a long golden chain with a blazing kick to Mia's belly spinning at the end of it.

Aa's trinity.

Mia hissed like she'd been scalded. Mister Kindly yowled, slithering away across the rooftops. The basilica bells started tolling the hour, joined by the countless other cathedrals across the City of Bridges and Bones. Mia dropped to her knees, puking. The agony of it almost made her scream, the sight of those three suns—white gold, rose gold, yellow gold—was blinding. She scrambled back against the bell tower, hands up to shield her eyes from that awful, burning light.

"Looks like the old tricks still work, then," Ashlinn said.

The bells fell silent, the rain still falling overhead. Ash looked about them, over the basilica's gutter to the drop below. Another novice of Aa was down in the courtyard now, pointing with his fellow at the girls on the roof.

"It's good to see you, Mia," Ash said softly.

"F-fuck . . . y-y—"

"I wondered if Drusilla would send you after me. I think out of all of them, you knew me best." Ash twirled the holy symbol around her finger. "Kept this, just in case. But you tell that crusty old bitch if she wants me dead, she can come herself. Because I'm surely coming for her. Her and all her merry fucking band."

Ash hung the medallion around her neck, rendered in silhouette against that awful, blistering hatred. The fury of a god, burning Mia blind.

"I'm sorry it was you, Mia," Ash sighed. "I always liked you. You're better than that place. Those murd—"

The dagger struck Ashlinn's shoulder. Blood sprayed, bright red between the raindrops. Ash twisted aside, another blade whistling past her cheek and chopping off a lock of her hair.

"Traitor!"

And as the blond curl fell, tumbling, turning toward the tiles, Jessamine dragged herself up over the guttering and flew at Ashlinn with her rapier drawn.

T he smell of hot food met them as they emerged from the cellar. Magistrae had met them in the bathhouse in exactly twenty minutes, carrying a bundle of new clothes. Not even Sidonius was fool enough to keep her waiting.

Once Mia had dressed in all she'd been given, she was tempted to ask where the rest of her outfit was. She wore a loincloth of padded gray linen, a leather belt to keep it in place. Her breasts were strapped with another strip of padded gray, leather sandals laced halfway up her shins. Her comrades wore even less—just loincloths and sandals for Sidonius and Matteo, with heavy leather cups to protect their dangles from the worst training might offer. The weather approaching truelight was so hot, the lack of material wouldn't bother anyone. But very little was being left to the imagination . . .

Sidonius wiggled his codpiece side to side. "I hear it's what all the marrowborn gentry are wearing in the 'Grave this year."

In a flash, a guard whipped out his truncheon and cracked it across the back of Sid's legs. The big man collapsed to his knees with a cry.

"For the last time, you will speak only when spoken to in my presence," Magistrae said. "Forget your place again, and I'll fashion you a worthy remembering. You can die on the sands just as well without a tongue in your head."

Sidonius grunted apology, and Mia helped the big man to his feet with a sigh. The big Itreyan wasn't the sharpest sword she'd ever met, but when living like a dog, you don't get to pick your fleas.

The houseguards escorted the trio upstairs to the verandah. The gladiatii were gathered at long benches, shoveling bowls of porridge home with all the appetite of folk who'd spent the turn sweating under the boiling suns. Magistrae nodded to a stick-thin man in a leather apron serving food. He had a crooked eye, a single circle marked on his cheek, and very few teeth in his head. Mia's mother had warned her never to trust a thin chef. But again, when living like a dog . . .

"Eat," Magistrae ordered, tossing her long gray braid over her shoulder. "You will need your strength amorrow."

Sidonius stalked toward the cook like a man at purpose, Mia and Matteo following. The girl realized she hadn't eaten since yestereve, but beneath her hunger, she still felt that cold queasiness from earlier in the afternoon. Scanning the faces of the gladiatii, she found Furian at the head of the first bench. The man had tied his long black hair back in a braid, speaking to the Dweymeri man between mouthfuls.

He glanced up as she entered, turned his gaze away just as swift. Questions burned in Mia's mind, backing up behind her teeth.

Patience.

She followed Sidonius to the porridge pot and snatched up a wooden bowl, almost drooling at the aroma. The thin man served a great, sloppy spoonful to Matteo.

"Oi, I was here first, you scrawny shit," Sidonius growled.

A meaty paw pushed the chef aside. Mia recognized the big Liisian gladiatii with a face like a dropped pie as he snatched the ladle. His head was shaved, only a tiny crop of dark hair remaining, like a cock's comb on his scalp. His face was pockmarked, his smile crooked—and not in the roguishly handsome sort of way. More in a dropped-one-too-many-times-on-his-head-as-a-babe kind of way.

"Pleasant turn to you, gentlefriends," he bowed. "Welcome to Remus Collegium."

Sidonius nodded greeting. "My thanks, brother."

Mia noted the other gladiatii all watching. Her hackles rising.

"O, think nothing of it," the pieman said. "Butcher, they name me. The Butcher of Amai." The Liisian looked them over with a smile. "Long journey from the Gardens? You must be hungrier than a breadline strumpet on the rag, neh?"

"Aye," Sidonius nodded. "We've not eaten since yesterturn."

"O, you'll find your needs well fixed presently. No better pigswill in all the Republic than's served by our domina." He rubbed his chin, thoughtful. "The porridge *can* be a touch bland, though. But no fear, I've just the spice."

The big Liisian reached into his loincloth with a grin. And without further ado, he whipped out his cock, and took a long noisy piss into the porridge pot.

The gladiatii erupted into howls of laughter, thumping the tables and calling Butcher's name. The big Liisian looked Mia square in the eye and he milked the last drops from his bladder, then turned back to Sidonius. His grin had evaporated utterly.

"You call me 'brother' again, I'll piss in your dinner and fucking drown you in it. My brothers and sisters under this roof are *gladiatii*." Butcher thumped his chest. "Until you last the Winnowing, you're *nothing*."

Butcher strode back to his meal, slapped on his back by several others. Mia stood with bowl in hand, the stench of fresh urine in her nostrils.

"I find myself not as hungry as I first thought," she confessed.

"Aye," Sidonius said. "We're of like mind, little Crow."

The trio found an empty bench, Mia and Sidonius staring while the other gladiatii ate their fill. After one look at their mournful expressions, Matteo scooped a spoonful of his own meal into Sidonius's bowl, another into Mia's. The big Itreyan watched in disbelief, Mia stared into Matteo's eyes.

"Are you certain?"

"Eat, Mi Dona," he smiled. "You'd do the same for me."

Mia shrugged, and she and Sidonius scoffed down the food without pause. The big mastiff wandered into the mess area, sniffing around on the floor for scraps. He mooched up to Matteo, eyeing his now empty bowl and wagging his stubby tail.

"Sorry friend," Matteo sighed. "If I had a crumb left, I'd share it."

Mia watched the boy sidelong as he patted the big dog, scruffing him behind his ears and grinning as his hind leg began thumping on the floor.

"His name is Fang," said a voice.

Mia looked up, saw the little girl named Maggot sitting in the rafters above their heads. Mia could remember climbing those some gables when she was a little girl, her mother scolding, her father applauding. That had ever been their way—Justicus Corvere indulging her tomboyish impulses, and the dona trying to sculpt her into a prize fit to marry off one turn. Mia wondered how her life might look if things had been different. Where she'd be if General Antonius had become king by her father's hand. Probably nowhere with a brand on her cheek and the stink of piss in her nose . . .

"Fang," Matteo smiled, patting the dog's shoulders. "A fine name."

"He likes you," the little girl said.

"I had hounds at home. I've a way with them."

He smiled wider, dark eyes sparkling. Too pretty for this place by far. But Maggot seemed to approve, ducking her head to hide her blush as she scrambled away.

With the meal finished, the gladiatii were marched down to the cellars. Mia, Sidonius and Matteo shuffled along in the rear, no word spoken to them that wasn't an order, no attention paid that wasn't a shove or a sneer. After only a handful of hours living at the bottom of the barrel, Mia found the novelty wearing thin. She wondered where Mister Kindly was, if he'd yet made it to Whitekeep and met—

"Looks like our champion is too good to sleep with the rest of us plebs," Sidonius muttered. "Effete wanker."

Mia followed the Itreyan's stare, saw Furian being escorted farther into the keep, instead of down to the barracks.

The Vaanian girl turned on Sid with a scowl.

"I'd watch that tongue of yours, Itreyan."

"Normally women offer to buy me a drink first," Sidonius grinned. "But, aye. You can watch it if please you, Dona. Where would you like me to put it?"

Mia rolled her eyes and sighed. The girl thrust her hand into Sidonius's codpiece, squeezing tight as he squeaked.

"Up your arsehole, you dopey fuck," she spat. "Furian the Unfallen is champion of this collegium. He sleeps apart from us, as is his right. You can speak ill of him when you best him in the *venatus*. Until then, shut your mouth, lest I shut it for you."

"Move!" barked the guard behind them.

The girl released her grip on Sidonius's jewels, stomped down the stairs. The big Itreyan sagged against Mia, and since she'd already kneed him in the dangles today, she was charitable enough to help him walk.

"You've certainly got a way with women, Sid," Matteo sighed, propping up the big Itreyan's other shoulder.

"J-just what your mother said," the big man winced.

The gladiatii gathered in the antechamber, and with a twist of that odd-key in the mekwork on the wall, the portcullis opened to the barracks beyond. Mia was led into a wide cell littered with fresh straw, Sidonius and Matteo behind her. Once each gladiatii was in their allotted cage, the guard in the antechamber outside flipped a lever. Each door slammed closed, the mekwerk locks thudded home, and in a moment, every warrior was secured behind a lattice of iron bars over three inches thick.

Now Mia saw the reason behind the dona letting her property sleep down here in the dark and the cool. It seemed for all her love of her precious "Falcons," Leona didn't want any of them flying their coop.

The arkemical lights burned low, the gladiatii talking among themselves out in the gloom. Mia listened to the warriors murmur, noting the blend of accents and timbres. The Dweymeri woman with the extensive tattoos had her own cell across the corridor, with genuine stone walls that offered some small privacy. Beneath the door, Mia could hear soft singing.

Without warning, the talk died, silence falling like fog. Mia heard a familiar *clink* thump, *clink* thump on the stone. She saw the towering figure of the executus limping among the cells, that hateful whip in his hand. His long salt-and-pepper hair was arranged about his shoulders like a mane, his beard freshly combed. That awful scar cut down his face, casting a long shadow across his features.

"I've been away from these walls too long, it seems," he growled. "If you've strength to sit up and chatter like maids at loom, you've obviously not been worked hard enough."

Passing by Mia's cell, he barely deigned to look at her. Executus limped back to the portcullis, blue eyes twinkling in the gloom.

"Rest your heads, Falcons," he called. "Tomorrow will be a long turn. I vow it."

The portcullis slammed shut with a mekwerk whine. Mia shook her head, mumbling under her breath. Sidonius grumbled too, voice thickened by his broken nose.

"I hope I get a chance in the circle with that bastard on the morrow. I'll knock his block off and fuck his corpse before it's cold."

"You'd need a cock for that, coward."

The barb came from across the corridor. Mia looked up to see Butcher, the Ruiner of Porridges, watching them from between the bars of his cage. His face was all bent nose and pockmarked skin, his body a patchwork of scar tissue.

Sidonius scowled at the gladiatii. "Call me coward again, I'll kill you and your whole fucking family."

"Talk, talk, little one," Butcher's lips twisted in an ugly smirk. "You'll see how much it avails you when you step into the circle with Executus."

"Pfft, you think I can't dance with a lame old dog like that?"

Butcher shook his head. "You're talking about one of the greatest gladiatii to walk the sand, you ignorant fool. He'll chew you up and use your bones for toothpicks."

Sidonius blinked. "Eh?"

"You never heard of the Red Lion of Itreya?"

"'Byss and blood." Mia looked to the gate Executus had left by. "*That's* Arkades?"

Matteo rubbed his eyes, sat up a little. "Who's Arkades?"

Butcher scoffed. "Clueless, the lot of them . . ."

"The Red Lion, they called him," Mia said.

". . . Executus used to be a slave like us?" Matteo asked.

"Not like you, you worthless shit," Butcher snarled. "He was fucking gladiatii."

"Victor of the *Venatus Magni* ten years back." Mia spoke softly, voice hushed with awe. "The Ultima was a free-for-all. Every gladiatii who'd been signed up for the games was released onto the sand for that final match. One warrior sent out every minute until the killing was done. Must've been almost two hundred."

"Two hundred and forty-three," Butcher said.

"And Executus killed them all?" Matteo breathed.

"Not by himself," Mia said. "But he was the last standing when the butchery was done. They say the sand in Godsgrave arena has never been the same color since."

"So they named him the Red Lion," Butcher said. "He won his freedom under Leonides's colors, see? Standing on a leg so badly broken, they had to cut it off afterward." He sneered at Sid. "Still want to dance with him, little man?"

Sidonius scowled, remained silent.

"I commanded you to *sleep*!" came the bellow from the portcullis.

Butcher sniffed, rolled over on his straw. Matteo did likewise, and after a few choice curses, Sid curled up with his back to them all. Mia sat brooding in the gloom.

The arkemical globes faded, their glow dying slow. Darkness fell in the barracks, only the faintest chinks of sunlight falling across the threshold from the stairs above. Mia felt it crawling across her scalp, goosebumps rising on her skin. The air down here was stifling, the stink of straw and sweat thick in the air. But at least it was dark.

It almost felt like home.

She waited an hour, until every chest rose and fell with the rhythm of slumber. Matteo murmuring. Sidonius snoring softly. Mia looked around the gloom, making sure each of her fellows was still. She closed her eyes. Held her breath and Stepped

out of the shadows

in her cell

and into the shadows

of the antechamber.

The room swam and she steadied herself against the wall. She could feel the heat of those two blazing suns in the sky above. Crouching low, she peered through the portcullis, back to the cells. And content her absence was unmarked, she stole like a whisper up into the keep.

Without Mister Kindly or Eclipse in her shadow, her heart was pounding, her palms damp with fear. She knew the building's layout like she knew her own name, but with no eyes to see except her own, she felt utterly alone. She could have waited until the shadowcat returned from Whitekeep with news, but her questions couldn't. Since the turn her father died, she'd wondered what she was. Now, all the answers might be only a heartbeat away . . .

She moved swift, all Shahiid Mouser's lessons ringing in her head. Listening for the tread of the houseguards who walked the lower levels. There was only one pair patrolling inside and it was easy enough to avoid them, sneaking through the silken curtains and ducking out of sight, making her way toward the kitchens.

She found them empty, the starving chef nowhere to be seen. But there was food aplenty in the larder and Mia dove in face-first, eating her fill. If she was to survive the Winnowing, she'd need every ounce of strength she could muster. She stole two steel forks, then slipped from the kitchens without a sound.

She dodged the patrol again, listening to the sickness in her belly and working her way by feel. She passed a long tapestry depicting the *venatus*—gladiatii clashing with fantastical beasts. Sets of gladiatii armor lined the hallway, sunslight glinting on crested helms and breastplates of polished steel. Fear rising now, churning in her belly as she reached a room with a barred slit, an iron lock.

And beyond it . . .

She took the two forks from her loincloth, bent the tines against the wall. Turning her ear for the guards, she knelt before the keyhole and set to work.

Soon enough, it popped open, the door came next, and with a glance over her shoulder for the guards, she stole inside.

Hands around her neck, twisting tight, flipping her over a broad shoulder and sending her crashing to the floor. Stars burst in her eyes as her skull cracked on the flagstones, an elbow jammed into her throat. She blinked up into a pair of glittering brown eyes, a handsome face framed by flowing locks of raven black.

Furian, the Unfallen.

He sat atop her, crushing the air from her lungs. This close, the gnawing sickness she felt in his presence was all-consuming, becoming less an illness and closer to a terrible hunger. But more pressing still was the need to breathe.

Mia pricked one of her forks into the champion's armpit. One good thrust and it'd slip over his ribcage and into the heart beyond. She tapped it against the hollow, trying not to sputter as Furian pressed his elbow farther into her larynx.

She pushed her steel harder, glaring wordlessly. And finally, Furian eased off, leaning back just enough to allow her to breathe.

His voice was deep and melodic. His eyes the brown of dark chocolate, delicious but edged with bitterness. Mia tried very hard not to notice that the body he pressed against her was utterly naked.

"What are you doing in here, slave?"

She put her free hand on his elbow, slowly pushed it aside.

"We need to talk," she replied. "Brother."

CHAPTER 10

SECRETS

Thunder split the skies as Ash and Jessamine clashed on the cathedral roof.

Both were soundless. No war cries or curses. No razored quips. Both had been trained in the art of death by the finest killers in the Republic, and both had marked their lessons well. Ashlinn drew two stilettos from her sleeves and met Jessamine's charge. Mia blinked through the falling rain, that awful burning light, noticing that Ash's weapons were discolored with poison. Though Jessamine had advantage with a longer blade, one scrape from Ash might be enough to end her.

Mia groped toward her longsword, tried to stand. But she could manage

neither—not with that accursed trinity around Ashlinn's throat. Every time Ash-
linn moved, the muted sunslight caught the medallion's face, lancing Mia's eyes.
Clenching her teeth, it was all she could do to hold back her whimper, let alone
stand and fight.

Mister Kindly had fled, and Eclipse couldn't approach the trinity either. Mia was
alone. Awful fear swelled in her belly, terror in the face of this god and his hatred.

All her power. All her training. All her gifts.

And she was utterly helpless.

Jessamine lunged across the slick tiles, the speed and feral cunning that had made
her Solis's favored pupil on display. Ash backed away, fear shining in her eyes as
she realized she was outmatched. But her voice was steady and cold.

"Nice to see you again, Jess. How's being second in line treating you?"

The bright notes of steel on steel.

The percussion of thunder.

"Tell me"—Ashlinn narrowly ducked Jessamine's strike—"how did it taste
when they teamed you up with the girl who cheated you out of becoming a Blade?"

Jessamine remained silent, refusing to be goaded. Pushing Ashlinn back, lung-
ing as her foe slipped on the rain-slick tile. Ashlinn scrambled back to her feet, losing
her grip on one of her knives. The poisoned dagger skittered down the roof's slope,
caught itself on the gutter's lip.

"How did it taste when Mia killed Diamo?"

Jessamine faltered for a moment, renewing her attack with furious intensity.
Ashlinn smiled, backing up closer to where Mia lay helpless. She held her poisoned
blade in front of her, deadlier poison dripping from her lips.

"Were you fucking him?" Ash asked. "I never found out. How did it taste bend-
ing the knee to the girl who murdered him?"

"Shut up," Jessamine whispered.

"He died messy, Jess," Ashlinn said. "Puking blood. Shit in his britches. Could
you smell it from the testing circle? I got a whiff from up in the bleachers."

"Shut up!"

Jessamine lunged, face twisted with rage. Ashlinn spun aside, and with her foe
off-balance, found time to reach into a belt pouch. Grasping a handful, flinging
out her hand, a bright flash of arkemical powder bursting in Jessamine's eyes. The
redhead staggered back, sputtering and blinded. Ashlinn closed for the kill, but
with her stomach seething, Mia lashed out with her boot, knocking Ashlinn's feet
out from under her.

Jessamine and Ashlinn went down together, rapier and poisoned blade both
clattering to the tiles. The girls fell to brawling, clawing at each other's faces, punch-
ing and kicking and cursing. They tumbled down the sloping roof, rolling to a halt

on the gutter's edge. Ashlinn lay underneath Jessamine, hands wrapped around the redhead's throat. Jessamine punched hard, splitting Ash's lip. Still half-blinded, she groped for Ash's collar, wrapping up the gold chain in her fist and strangling back. The chain snapped clean, the trinity dropping thirty feet onto the cobbles below. Thunder rolled, lightning tearing across the skies as the medallion fell out of sight, the pain in Mia's skull, the sickness in her belly slowly fading.

"*You fucking traitor,*" *Jessamine spat, punching Ash in the jaw.*

"*Get . . . off m-me!*"

"*I'll show you what dying messy looks like.*"

Jessamine wrapped her fingers around Ash's throat, punched her again with her free hand. She was raising her fist to strike again when a voice rose above the storm.

"*Jess, th-that's enough.*"

The redhead refused to look over her shoulder, bloodshot eyes locked on Ashlinn. Mia was on her feet, not looking anything close to steady, but slowly making her way down the roof with her gravebone longsword in hand.

"*Fuck you, Corvere,*" *Jessamine spat.*

"*We n-need her alive.*" *Mia spit the taste of vomit off her tongue.* "*She double-crossed the braavi. But they p-paid a fortune. There's no way she just incinerated a map that valuable. Presuming she even has it, we can't find it if she's dead.*"

"*I don't take orders from you.*"

Mia sighed. "*You're my Hand, Jess. That's exactly what you do.*"

Jessamine turned to glare at Mia, sodden hair in her eyes. Her frustration, the rage of the past seven nevernights in Mia's company finally getting the better of her.

"*I should be delivering this offering. I should be the Blade here, not you.*"

"*Nobody said life was fair, Red.*"

"*Fair?*" *Jessamine laughed.* "*Who the f—ckkkg . . .*"

Jessamine reeled backward, blood gushing from her throat. Ashlinn stabbed the girl again, the poisoned blade that had fallen into the gutter flashing in her hand. Jessamine gasped, hands to her punctured neck, arterial red spraying between her fingers and down her sodden tunic. Ashlinn stabbing again. And again.

Mia roared Jess's name as thunder crashed, as Ashlinn grabbed the Hand's collar and slung her forward. Jessamine clutched Ash's wrist in desperation, trying to stop her fall. But with a sickening crunch, the girl toppled off the roof and onto the fence bordering the basilica grounds, impaled on the wrought-iron spikes below.

The novices below cried out in horror, ran screaming for the Luminatii, for the cardinal, for anyone. Arcs of jagged blue white lit the skies as Ashlinn dragged herself to her feet, soaked with Jessamine's blood.

"You bitch," Mia whispered.

Ashlinn wiped her knuckles across split lips. Pawing at her throat, she realized the trinity was gone.

"Mia, you don't understand what's happening here . . ."

Mia raised her blade. "You killed her."

Blood soaking Ashlinn's hands.

Rage swimming in Mia's eyes.

Lightning reflected on the pale edge of her longsword, in the empty gaze of the dead girl hanging on the wrought-iron fence below their feet.

The basilica bells started ringing again—a warning this time. Acolytes were gathered in the courtyard below, howling, "Murder! Murder!" Mia stepped forward, blade poised. With the trinity over the edge of the building, Mister Kindly and Eclipse had returned, filling the terrifying emptiness she'd felt with the strength of cold steel. Ash's feet were snared in her own shadow—she had nowhere to run. But Mia had spoken truth to Jessamine; if she killed the girl now, she'd not see that map. And after her last flaying before the Ministry, she'd be damned if she returned to them empty-handed.

But if she returned with the girl who'd brought the Ministry to their knees?

Black Mother, imagine the look on Solis's face . . .

So, Mia drew back her sword and cracked the crow hilt across Ashlinn's jaw. The girl tumbled onto her backside, half-senseless. Mia set about searching Ash's clothing, boots, sleeves, finding blades and toxins and arkemical powders and hurling them off the roof. Ashlinn sat up, dazed, and Mia pressed her sword tip into the flesh above the girl's heart. She could hear the faint sound of heavy boots over the thunder.

". . . luminatii, mia . . ."

". . . GOD-BOTHERING CURS. LET THEM COME . . ."

". . . so eager for blood, dear mongrel . . . ?"

". . . SO EAGER TO RUN, LITTLE MOGGY . . . ?"

"I appreciate the sentiment, Eclipse," Mia whispered. "But living to fight another turn is probably the goal here."

The shadowwolf growled grudging assent, and Mia turned to Ashlinn.

"Right. You can get off this roof two ways. Feet or face first?"

"Is . . . this a t-trick question?"

Mia dug the razored point of her blade into Ashlinn's skin. Gravebone was harder than steel, sharp enough to bleed stone. One soft push . . .

"You try to make a break, or even breathe in a way I don't like, we paint the cobbles an interesting shade of Ashlinn. Are we clear?"

". . . mia, we must go . . ."

The blade twitched. "Clear?"

Ash winced. "As Dweymeri crystal."

Mia slipped her belt from around her waist. "Hold out your wrists."

"Didn't know you were so inclined," Ash smirked. "Honestly, all you n—"

The blade sank deeper, and Ashlinn winced in pain. With a hurt glance, she offered her wrists. Mia looped the belt around them, cinching tight. She could hear the legionaries clearly now, a multitude of citizens gathered beyond the cathedral gates, looking in horror at Jessamine's dangling corpse.

Mia stood, pulled on the leather strap.

"Move."

She led Ashlinn to a downspout behind the bell tower. A gargoyle spewed rainwater from its mouth into the churchyard two stories below.

"Traitors first," Mia insisted.

"Going to be hard climbing with my hands tied, neh?"

"You'll manage. And don't even think about running when you hit the floor. Throwing knives run quicker than you, and I'm carrying six in your size."

Ash scowled, but for all her moaning, shimmied down the spout without much trouble. Mia followed, Mister Kindly whispering urgent warnings in her ear. The girls ran across the basilica grounds, past a necropolis littered with familia tombs. They vaulted the iron fence as a troop of Luminatii rounded the cathedral, shouted, "Halt!" Mia snatched the belt around Ash's wrists, dragging her captive into the streets.

The legionaries were wearing steel breastplates and carrying burning sunsteel longswords, but they vaulted that fence quicker than Mia would've given them credit for—a murder on Aa's holy ground was no chucklefest for his faithful. Mia looked at the crowd around her, pausing to snatch the full braavi purse from Ashlinn's belt.

"Corvere, don't you fucking d—"

Mia slung the bag in a wide arc, scattering a shower of glittering gold into the mob. The reaction was instantaneous, astonishingly violent, the people around them erupting as they realized the sky had somehow rained a living fortune. People flocked into the street from the taverna and stores all around, beggars, bakers, butchers, cutting off the cadre of Luminatii and punching and shouting and kicking over Ashlinn's gold.

Ashlinn wailed as Mia dragged her away through the driving rain. They dashed over a broad bridge, into the warrens behind the administratii buildings, and there, finally, Mia pulled Ashlinn into a small alcove.

"Do you realize how much—"

"Shut up," Mia hissed. Reaching out to the shadows around them, Mia plucked

them with clever fingers, twisting and weaving them into a mantle about her shoulders. With a flick of her wrist, she enveloped Ashlinn as well, just as she'd done the turn they stole into Speaker Marius's chambers. Memories of their turns in the Red Church made Mia think of Jessamine, the sight of the Hand's body dangling from those wrought-iron spikes burned in her mind's eye.

Jess, Tric, every Blade murdered in the Luminatii pogrom, the capture of the Ministry . . . Ashlinn was responsible for all of it. The girl in her arms might as well have been a snake, coiled and ready to strike.

"Not a sound," Mia whispered, pressing her gravebone blade to Ash's throat.

All the world was black beneath Mia's cloak, but she still heard the legionaries shouting to each other as they searched the Godsgrave backstreets. The girls waited, pressed against each other beneath Mia's shadows for endless minutes.

A whisper finally rose over the pattering rain.

". . . they are gone, mia . . ."

Ashlinn swallowed against the blade at her throat. "You kill me now, I swear by the Mother you're never going to see that map they've got you chasing."

"Good thing I'm not going to kill you, then," Mia said. "Mister Kindly, you check the rooftops. Eclipse, you scout ahead, make sure the way back to the chapel is clear."

". . . SO BE IT. BUT IF YOU MURDER ANYONE WHILE I AM GONE, I WILL BE MOST UPSET . . ."

She felt the shadows about her ripple, the not-cat and not-wolf slipping from the dark at her feet. Mister Kindly flitted up the wall, shadow to shadow, Eclipse spilling across the cobbles and off into the street. She could feel Ash's heart beating, smell a faint perfume of lavender and fresh sweat on her skin.

"You're taking me back to the chapel?" the girl asked.

"There's a dose of Swoon on the blade at your throat, Ash. I don't much fancy knocking you out and carrying you back, but I will if must. Now, shut the fuck up."

"They've been hunting me for eight months. They get their hands on m—"

"You can count the shits I give on no hands, Ashlinn."

"I didn't want to kill Tric, Mia."

Ashlinn winced as Mia pushed her gravebone stiletto up under her chin.

"Don't you dare say his name."

Ashlinn raised her hands, spoke slow and careful. Mia could hear the fear in her voice, the slight tremble that told her that, for all Ash's front, the girl didn't want to die.

"I wanted the Ministry, Mia. Anyone else was just wrong place, wrong time."

"Including your own brother?"

"So. It was you that killed Osrik."

"No," Mia replied. "But only because Marius ended him before I got the chance. The pair of you killed Tric. You betrayed your vows. You betrayed the Church."

"To avenge my father! You of all people should understand that."

"Don't push your luck, Ashlinn." Mia tightened her grip. "My father is dead."

"Aye?" Ash snarled. "Well, so is mine."

That gave Mia pause. Unspoken questions hanging in the air. The rain was dying now, the skies still a sullen gray. Ashlinn drew a long ragged breath.

"We dodged the Church and their Blades for eight months," she murmured. "They finally caught us in Carrion Hall. My father was good. One of the finest Blades to ever serve the Black Mother. But everyone's luck runs out eventually."

Mia simply shook her head, refusing to bite. Ashlinn Järnheim was made of lies. She'd lied all through their training at the Church. She'd lied to the Ministry, to Mia, to everyone she ever met. She'd struck at the heart of Jessamine on the basilica roof, she was striking at Mia's heart now. Every word she spoke was poison.

"I'm not going to tell you to shut up again, Ash."

Ashlinn sighed, her temper fraying. "You have no fucking idea what's going on here, do you? I know you, Mia. Do you have any idea what the Red Church actually is? Do you think they're ever going to let you kill Scaeva when he pays their wages?"

Mia felt the consul's name like a fist in her belly.

"You're full of shit."

"Why do you think Scaeva isn't dead already? Half the Senate want him in the ground, you think they couldn't afford to hire a Blade to do him over if he wasn't protected by Sanctity? Julius Scaeva is a fucking bastard, but he's not a fucking fool. He's been a patron of the Church for years."

"They'd never—"

"They're assassins, of course they would! There's no sanctity to what the Red Church does. They murder people for money. Half of them are psychopaths and the rest are just sadistic bastards. They're not servants of some divine Goddess of Night, they're fucking whores."

Mia's mind was racing. She knew nothing Ash said could be trusted . . . but somewhere in her words, Mia could hear the ring of truth. People who posed a threat to Scaeva either got killed like her father, or bought like the braavi. Wouldn't it make sense he'd buy the Church, too? Why else would they order her Scaeva wasn't to be touched?

"How do you know all this?" she asked.

"Because I'm a sneaky bitch, Mia."

"You're a lying cunt is what you are."

"There's an obsidian vault inside the Revered One's chambers," Ash spat. "And inside that vault, they keep a ledger of every offering the Church has undertaken. All their patrons. All their shit. When I poisoned the Ministry at the initiation feast, I stole the ledger, Mia. That's the reason they've been hunting me and my da for the past eight months. Not because we betrayed them. Because we know all their dirty little secrets."

Ashlinn turned her head a little, despite the blade at her throat. Just so she could look into Mia's eyes.

"Including the one about you and your father."

Ashlinn fell silent as Mia pressed her blade back against her throat. Ash killed Jessamine. She'd killed Tric. Mia knew she'd do anything, say anything to avoid being taken back to the chapel.

"You're a liar," Mia said.

"I am at that. But not about this, Mia. If you take me back to the Church, they're going to kill me, and you'll never know the truth of what they did."

"And I'm just supposed to take you at your word on all this?"

"You can see for yourself."

". . . You have the ledger?"

"Something tells me names on a page aren't going to sway you. But I can tell you exactly where you need to go to find proof written in something more than ink."

"O, aye? And where would that be exactly?"

Ashlinn looked up at Mia, blue eyes glittering like broken sapphires.

"Back to Church."

W e have nothing to talk about," Furian spat.

Mia was still sprawled underneath the Champion of the Remus Collegium, his forearm against her throat. Muscle rippling in his arm, across his chest. She pressed her fork into Furian's ribs again, hard enough now to break the skin.

"I'm not sure about the other women you've known," she said softly, "but I don't much fancy it on my back. Let me up."

"I should knock your teeth out for even talking to me. How did you get in here?"

"Let. Me. Up. Fucker."

Furian glanced to his now unlocked door. Mia had no idea of the consequences if they were discovered in each other's company, but she doubted they'd be pleasant. She could hear the guard patrol, slowly coming closer.

With a curse, Furian twisted off Mia, pushed the door closed. He listened for a moment, ear to the wood as the guards passed by. Mia looked the champion up and down, skin prickling in spite of herself. She'd never seen a man quite like him, all hard tanned skin and rippling muscle. But there was a speed to him, also. Lithe and fierce, like a big cat. His body was utterly hairless—shaved, she supposed, to show off his physique to the adoring crowds. His jaw was strong, the rivers and valleys of his abdomen leading her eyes down, chewing her lip as she drank in the sight of him.

She'd no idea what had come over her. Though she'd found Lord Cassius attractive, her reaction to his presence hadn't been quite as . . . carnal. Perhaps because she'd never been quite this close to the Lord of Blades? Perhaps because she'd been younger? Whatever the reason, looking at Furian now, she found her breath coming quicker. Thighs aching. Waves of butterflies thrilling her belly.

His chamber was sparsely adorned. A small barred window looked out over the ocean, a simple bed stood against the wall, a practice dummy and wooden swords in another corner. A small shrine to Tsana, First Daughter of the Everseeing and patron of warriors, sat beneath the window, and the three interlocking circles of Aa's trinity were scribed on the wall in charcoal. Though it was only trinities blessed by Aa's truest believers that made her feel ill, the sight of the holy symbol was still a little unsettling.

All in all, Furian's accommodations were hardly a marrowborn villa. But compared to the barracks, they were positively palatial. And better, private.

When the guards had passed beyond earshot, the champion turned to Mia. His jaw was clenched. Long dark hair framing those delicious chocolate eyes.

"You feel it, don't you?" Mia breathed.

Furian stalked across the room and snatched up a strip of gray linen from the bed, wrapped it around his waist to make himself decent.

"Feel what?"

Mia pulled herself up off the floor, dragged her hair behind her ear. She saw movement from the corner of her eye, glanced to the shadows cast on the wall by the shrine's candlelight. Hers. His.

"Maw's teeth," she breathed. "Look . . ."

Their shadows were moving of their own accord.

Hair blowing as if in some hidden breeze, ebbing and flowing toward each other like waves on a lonely shore. Mia's shadow reached toward Furian's, though in the flesh, the girl hadn't moved a muscle. The Unfallen reached out and touched the wall, as if to test if his shadow were real. But his shadow didn't move as he did, instead reaching out toward Mia's.

The champion stumbled back, held up three fingers—Aa's warding sign against evil. And at that, the shadows fell still, trembling only for the candle flame.

"You're like me," Mia said.

Furian blinked, turned away from the shadows to look at Mia.

"I am nothing like you," he growled. "I am gladiatii."

"I mean you're *darkin,*" Mia said. "Just as I am."

"I say again, I am nothing like you, girl."

"Where is your passenger?"

". . . My what?"

"Your daemon," Mia said. "I have two who live in my shadow. Usually, anyway. What shape does yours wear? And where is it?"

"I know of no daemon," he growled, "save the one standing before me now."

He looked her up and down, something close to disgust on his face. But she could see goosebumps rising on his skin, just as they did on hers. He was breathing harder, his pupils dilated—all the telltale marks Shahiid Aalea had taught her to recognize in a man. Or woman.

Want.

"How did you escape your cell?" he demanded.

Mia shrugged. "I Stepped between the shadows."

"Witchery," he spat.

"It's not witchery. It's what we *are.* Can you not do the same?"

"I'll hold no truck with the darkness." Furian raised the warding sign again.

"But you already did," she said, stepping toward him. "This very turn on the sands, when I fought Executus. You stopped me from—"

"Get out of here, girl. I am champion of this collegium, and a god-fearing son of Aa. Gladiatii do not mix with chaff, and I do not mix with heretics."

Mia glanced at the shrine to Tsana, the trinity of Aa on the wall.

Could it be?

". . . You're of the faithful? How can you—"

"Get *out,*" he hissed. He dared not raise his voice lest the guards overhear, but Mia could see the fury in his clenched fists, the tendons taut at his neck. "If the guards find you in my cell, Executus will see the skin peeled off both our backs. And I'll not bleed for the likes of you. Now begone before I snap your neck and take my chance with the domina's mercy."

His shadow seethed across the wall, hands extended toward her own shadow's throat. Mia stepped back, but her shadow remained unmoved, its hair twisting and coiling like a nest of snakes. The hunger surged inside her again, the sickness, mixed now with a dull, seething anger.

This man didn't know anything about darkin. Didn't know anything about himself. There were no answers here. Only more questions.

And the longer she stayed in his room, the more likely she'd be caught.

Mia retreated slowly, not turning her back, listening for the guards at the door. Hearing nothing, she opened it without a sound, checking that the corridor beyond the chamber was clear. Satisfied, she looked back over her shoulder to the champion of the collegium, his shadow flickering upon the wall.

She reminded herself of why she was here. To stand as victor in the *magni*, she'd have to best this man, darkin or no. And whatever dark kinship she might have with him came second to the knowledge that he stood between her and victory.

Her and vengeance.

So be it.

"This is a nice room," she noted, looking about the chamber.

"What of it?" Furian spat.

Mia shrugged.

"I'd not get too comfortable in it if I were you."

The girl slipped out the door, closing it behind her.

It took a few heartbeats for her shadow to follow.

C*rack!*

"Gladiatii fear nothing, save defeat!"

Crack!

"Gladiatii thirst for nothing, save victory!"

Crack!

"Gladiatii live for nothing, save glory!"

Such was the tune of Mia's hours, sweltering beneath the blistering suns. Executus's voice was the verse, the snap of his whip the beat, and the grunts and sighs and curses of the men and women around her the chorus.

A week had passed since she'd arrived at Crow's Nest, but those seven turns had seemed long as years. Executus showed no mercy, drilling her and Matteo and Sidonius in every weapon, every fighting form, every trick and twist his years in the games had taught him. They sparred in the circle, on the uneven levels across the yard, in their sleep. Every stumble was met by his whip. Every misstep. Every slight.

Crack!

Crack!

Crack!

They'd been kept apart from the gladiatii, bathed and fed last. Butcher had spoiled at least three more of their evemeals, twice with piss, and once with a handful of dogshit he'd fetched after Fang had done his business in the yard. Mia had stolen food every nevernight in shadow jaunts to the kitchens, once had even managed to sneak some bread to Sidonius and Matteo with the excuse she'd found it in the mess hall. But she was still worn thin. Her fellow recruits were in even worse shape.

"You worthless whorespawn!" Executus roared at the trio. "In a few turns, you step onto the sands of the *venatus* under the colors of this collegium. If you think the crowd will not howl for more when they see the first drop of your blood, you are greater fools than I gave credit for. Now, attack with purpose!"

"Executus?" came a call from above.

Mia looked up, saw Dona Leona standing on the broad balcony above. She was dressed in rippling white silk, gold at her wrists, auburn hair plaited down her back.

"Attend!" Executus roared.

The gladiatii fell still, thumping fists to chest.

"Domina?" Executus asked.

The woman crooked a finger and beckoned.

"Your whisper, my will," the big man bowed.

He turned to Mia and her fellows.

"Sidonius, work the woodmen." He glared at Mia and Matteo. "You two, spar in the circle. You still carry a shield like a parcel of posies, girl. And Matteo wields a sword like a three-year-old swings his pecker. If you want to keep those pretty heads on your shoulders during the Winnowing, the pair of you had best get to toiling."

Executus stroked his beard, limped away into the keep. Sidonius set to work on the training dummies, Maggot fetched Mia and Matteo some wooden swords and shields, and they set to sparring, clashing in the dust and dancing around the circle.

"Get to toiling?" Matteo spat. "What the 'byss does he think we've been doing all week?"

Mia made no reply, intent on training. Despite being an utter bastard, now that she knew the executus was Arkades, she hung on his every word. If the Red Lion told her to work her shield arm, then Black Mother, she was going to work her fucking shield arm.

"Strike harder," she growled. "Press me."

"I am!" Matteo spat, stabbing at her with his blade.

Mia fended off his blows with ease, and a flurry of strikes sent the boy skipping back across the sand. She battered his shield again, spitting dust off her tongue.

"'Byss and blood, you're swinging at me like I'm made of glass. Hit me!"

Matteo blocked another blow, countered with a weak riposte. Wooden blades cracked against wooden shields, their feet dancing to the frantic percussion.

"I don't want to hurt you, Crow," Matteo said.

"And why not? Because I might hurt you back?"

"Because . . . you're a girl," he said.

Mia's eyes widened at that. Gritting her teeth, she wove past Matteo's strike, sandals scuffing in the dust. Spinning on the spot, she smacked him hard across his shoulder blades, sent him staggering. As he turned to face her, she clocked him in the face with her shield, blood spraying as he toppled onto the dirt.

Mia stood over him, pressing her wooden blade to his throat.

"Take hold of your fucking jewels," she said. "Maybe your mother raised you to treat us all as delicate flowers, maybe you're just thinking with your cock. But there *are* no girls on the sand. No mothers or daughters. Sons or fathers. Only *enemies*. You spend a moment worrying about what's between your opponent's legs, you'll find your head parted from your body. And what good will your fool cock do you then?"

The boy wiped the blood from his face, swallowing thick.

"Forgiveness," he muttered. "I d—"

"Gladiatii! Attend!"

Mia turned from Matteo's bloodied face to the balcony. She saw Executus Arkades, Dona Leona beside him. The woman smiled like the suns, spoke with a loud, clear voice.

"My Falcons! Tomorrow we set out for Blackbridge and the grand games held in honor of Governor Salvatore Valente! This is the second official event of the *venatus* season, and all eyes will be upon it. Remus Collegium now stands in high regard, thanks to the victory of our champion in Talia last month."

Here she took in Furian with a wave of her hand. The gladiatii roared his name, pounded swords upon shields.

"But Furian's triumph has not assured our berth in the *magni*!" Leona continued. "The crowds are ever hungry for blood, and the editorii seek only the finest for their grand spectacle. We must have victory. We *will* have victory!"

"Victory!" they cried.

"The following gladiatii have earned the right to attend the Blackbridge *venatus* and fight for the Falcons of Remus. Step forward, Butcher of Amai!"

The Ruiner of Porridges stepped forward with his dropped-as-a-babe smile, raising the knuckles to the men behind him.

"Bladesinger, the Reaper of Dweym!"

The woman with the full-body tattoos stepped forward and bowed.

"Our equillai, Byern and Bryn, shall once again thrill the crowd!"

The blond Vaanian siblings bowed low. Looking closer at the pair side by side, Mia marked them for twins—they were simply too alike to be otherwise.

"Our legend of the sands, the mightiest Falcon in this collegium, victor of Talia, Furian, the Unfallen!"

The champion strode forward to the cheers of his fellows, twin blades in hand. His eyes were fixed on the balcony as he bowed deep, long black hair spilling around his high cheekbones, his square jaw. Mia looked to his shadow and saw nothing of note. But her own rippled slightly, like still water when a stone is dropped into it.

"And finally," Leona called. "Our three new recruits will wager their lives in the Winnowing, earning their place among you or perishing in the attempt. Pray that Aa grants them favor, that Tsana guides their hands to victory." Leona looked among her flock, opened her arms. *"Sanguii e Gloria!"*

"Sanguii e Gloria!" came the cry.

Mia listened to them call, fists raised high, crying out for blood and glory. In truth, she wanted nothing to do with the latter. Blood was her intent, her dream, her only prize. Cardinal Duomo and Scaeva within arm's reach on the victor's podium. But to stand before them, she needed to accrue victories enough to secure a place in the *magni*. And somehow, in the midst of that bloodbath and butchery, she had to win.

The gladiatii around her looked to the sky, called to Aa and his firstborn to bring them victory. But Mia had no use for the Everseeing, nor his warrior daughter. Aa had only ever proved her enemy, and Tsana had never helped her before.

Why would she start now?

And so, Mia turned her eyes to the sand. To the shadow, black and pooled around her feet. Wondering if the goddess would answer after all she'd done.

All she'd undone.

Wondering if prayers would help her at all.

"Black Mother," she whispered. "Give me strength."

THUNDER

Mia emerged from Marius's pool with a gasp.

Blood in her eyes and on her tongue, thudding in her temples. Standing naked in the pool, she looked at the speaker at its apex. Pale skin and paler hair, his lips twisted in a small smile. He opened his eyes, the whites slicked with red.

"Thou hast returned, Blade Mia. Thy quarry dead, thy offering complete?"

"Not yet."

Marius tilted his head, smiling wider. "Missed me then, didst thou?"

Mia turned her back, waded up out of the pool, feeling the speaker's eyes roaming her curves. Dripping red on the stone, she headed to the baths to wash the gore off, sinking below the water with a sigh.

". . . i do not like this, mia . . ."

Mister Kindly sat at the corner of her bath, watching with his not-eyes.

"Nor I. But what choice do I have?"

". . . ashlinn is a liar, and we are fools to trust her . . ."

"We don't trust her. Eclipse is watching her."

". . . i do not trust eclipse, either . . ."

She dried off, wrapped herself in black leathers and velvet, picturing Ash as she'd left her; chained to a four-poster bed in a cheap Godsgrave inn, a wolf made of shadows poised over her, translucent fangs bared. Eclipse couldn't actually touch the girl, of course. But Mia didn't feel any particular need to tell Ashlinn that . . .

". . . she is leading you by the nose, mia . . ."

"You think I don't suspect that? I'm not a fucking idiot, Mister Kindly. But what if she's telling the truth?"

". . . then we will find ourselves in interesting waters . . ."

"I have to know . . ."

The shadowcat sighed.

". . . i know. and i am with you, mia. do not be afraid . . ."

She checked the gravebone blade at her belt, the other in her sleeve.

"Not with you beside me."

She stole out from the bathhouse, into the Red Church's gloom. The hymns of the ghostly choir hung in the air as she made her way up winding stairs and down corridors of black stone, carved with patterns of endless spirals. Naev had once told her the patterns in the walls were a song about finding her way in the dark. Thinking about all Ashlinn had told her, she found herself wishing she knew the words. If the girl had spoken true, Mia would be utterly lost.

It can't be true.

On through the hungry dark.

It can't be . . .

Up coiling stair and down twisting spiral until she reached it.

The Hall of Eulogies.

She looked up at the towering statue of Niah, her sword and scales in hand. It might have been a trick of the light, but the goddess looked grimmer than usual.

Mia's footsteps echoed in the silent hall as she walked the periphery, brushing her fingertips over the empty tomb marked with Tric's name. She thought of her friend then. The counsel he'd given. The comfort she'd found in his arms. He'd been a rock in a world growing more uncertain by the nevernight . . .

"You miss him," came a voice.

Mia turned, saw Shahiid Aalea standing in the archway, dark eyes glittering. She was dressed in sheer, bloody red, the same color as her lips. Black curls tumbled about her shoulders, her skin alabaster pale. A woman like her could have seemed cold as wintersdeep in the wrong light. But Aalea's smile was as warm as a glass of goldwine.

"Shahiid," Mia said, bowing low.

"You return." Dark eyes flitted over Mia's face. "Absent victory, by the look."

"I needed a nevernight back in my own bed," Mia said. "But the Dona is dead. And the map is almost within my grasp."

"You'd rather the boy there instead, I'll wager?"

Aalea nodded to Tric's empty tomb. Mia stared too, saying nothing. The Shahiid ran fingertips over Tric's name, carved in the stone.

"You miss him?" she asked.

Mia saw no sense in denying it.

"Not like a piece of me is gone." She shrugged. "But aye. I do."

Aalea pursed her lips, as if uncertain to speak.

"I loved someone once," she finally said. "Thinking this place, this life I chose, could not sully what I knew to be so pure." The Shahiid ran her fingers across her lips. "I loved that man as the Night loved the Day. I promised him we'd be together forever."

"What happened?" Mia asked.

"He died," Aalea sighed. "Death is the only promise we all keep. This life we

live . . . there is room in it for love, Mia. But a love like autumn leaves. Beautiful one turn. A bonfire the next. Only ashes the remainder."

Mia was quietened by the picture Aalea conjured. Eyes to the tombs. She'd no wish to raise suspicion, but the last thing in the world she wanted was to stand here talking about love and loss with a mass murderer. Not if what Ashlinn had told her was anything close to true . . .

"Did you think one turn you might find yourself beside a happy hearth?" Aalea asked. *"With a beau at your side and grandchildren on your knee?"*

". . . I'm not sure what I supposed anymore."

"Such is not the lot of a Blade," Aalea took Mia's hand, pressing it to her lips. *"But there is beauty in knowing all things end, Mia. The brightest flames burn out the fastest. But in them, there is warmth that can last a lifetime. Even from a love that only lasts the nevernight. For people like us, there are no promises of forever."*

Mia looked to the statue above. Those eyes that followed wherever she walked. *"My father used to say the art of telling a good story lies in knowing when to stop. Keep talking long enough, you'll find there's no such thing as a happy ending."*

Aalea smiled. *"A wise man."*

Mia shook her head. Remembering the way he died. What he died for.

"Not that wise."

Ashlinn's words ringing in her ears. Her jaw clenched.

Aalea looked again to Tric's empty tomb.

"He would have made a fine Blade," she sighed. *"And he was a beauty. But he is gone. Do not allow your sorrows to stray you from your path, Mia."*

Mia looked Aalea deep in the eye. Her voice was iron.

"I know my path, Shahiid. Sometimes, sorrow is all that keeps me on it."

Aalea smiled, sweet and dark as chocolate.

"Forgive me. An old teacher's habits die hard, I suppose. You are a Blade, for now. And a woman. And a beauty at that." Aalea leaned closer, eyes locked on Mia's, lips just a breath from her own. *"I have been ever fond of you. Know if ever you seek counsel, it is yours. And if ever you wish to build a bonfire to keep you warm one nevernight, I am here."*

Mia's pulse ran quicker, skin prickling. This close, she could smell the rose and honey of the Shahiid's perfume. Staring into those dark, kohl-smudged eyes, she wondered again if there was some arkemy at work in Aalea's scent, or if . . .

Eyes on the prize, Corvere.

Mia slipped her hand free of Aalea's. Licked at suddenly dry lips.

"My thanks, Shahiid," she murmured. *"I'll think on it."*

"I am certain you will, love," Aalea said, her smile deepening. *"But now, I*

*will leave you to your memories. Do not let the Revered Father find you here ab-
sent quarry, unless you actually enjoy hearing him bluster."*

The Shahiid of Masks inclined her head and drifted out of the room, leaving
her perfume hanging in the air. Mia watched her go, the pull of the woman almost dragging her off-balance. But knowledge of why she was here tempered all,
crushing the butterflies in her belly. She felt her shadow ripple, the dark swelling
at her feet.

". . . dangerous, that one . . ."

"*The same could be said of every woman I know.*"

". . . where to begin . . . ?"

"*You start at this end and head inward. I'll begin at the Mother's feet. Keep
an ear out for company. We've need of none.*"

". . . you do not honestly expect this search to bear fruit . . ."

"*I don't know what to expect anymore. Let's be about it.*"

Mia crouched at the foot of Niah's statue, and in the light of that bloody stained
glass, she began searching the names carved into the stone. One by one. Thousands
of them. A spiral, coiling out from the goddess's feet. The names of kings, senators,
legates, lords. Priests and sugargirls, beggars and bastards. The names of every life
taken in the service of the Black Mother.

The choir and Mister Kindly were her only company, and she worked in
silence. Wondering what she would do if all Ashlinn had told her was true. Once
or twice she was forced to hide herself beneath her cloak of shadows as a Hand or
new acolytes wandered through the hall. But for the most part, she was uninter-
rupted, on her knees in the dark as the names of the dead blurred together inside
her head.

She remembered the turn he died. Her father. Standing before the noose and
the baying mob. Cardinal Duomo on the scaffold, hedgerow beard and broad
shoulders. Julius Scaeva standing above, with his jet-black hair and his deep, dark
eyes and his consul's robes dipped in purple and blood. There to watch the leaders
of the rebellion executed for their crimes against the great Itreyan Republic. Justicus Darius Corvere and General Gaius Antonius had gathered an army, set to
march it upon their own capital. But on the eve of the invasion had come salva-
tion, the rebel leaders delivered into the Republic's hands.

Mia had been too young to ask. And then, too blinded to wonder.

But how?

How had the leaders of the rebellion fallen into the Senate's clutches, when they
were safely ensconced within an armed camp? Antonius was no fool. Mia's father,
neither. It would have taken God himself to breach their defenses and steal them
away.

God. Or perhaps someone in service to a goddess . . .

"*. . . mia . . .*"

She looked up at the tone in Mister Kindly's voice, pupils dilating in the dark.

"*. . . o, mia . . .*"

She scuttled across the floor to where the shadowcat stood. Searching the names carved in the granite. Her father and Antonius had been hanged before the Godsgrave mob—even if the Red Church had something to do with their capture, they hadn't actually killed them. But if others fell during their capture, then perhaps . . .

Mia's belly turned to greasy ice.

"*'Byss and blood," she whispered.*

Carved in the stone, just as Ashlinn promised. A single name among the thousands. The name of a slave who purchased his freedom, and yet remained by her father's side afterward. Darius Corvere's right hand. His majordomo. A man who would have been with his justicus as he prepared to march on his own capital. A man who would have been with her father until the end.

Andriano Varnese.

"*. . . it is true, then . . .*"

Cold ice in her belly as her fingers traced the name in the stone.

Ashes and dust in her mouth.

The Red Church had a hand in her father's capture. The rebellion's failure. Why else would the name of her father's majordomo be carved here on the stone? How else would a general and his justicus be captured in the middle of ten thousand men?

All this time, she'd been training in a den of murderers to avenge herself on the men who'd executed her father. Never imagining for a moment that the murderers she trained with played a role in that same execution.

And all at the behest of the man she wished to murder most of all.

Ash had spoken truth.

All of it. Everything.

Undone in a moment.

"*O, Goddess," Mia breathed.*

She looked to the statue above her. The sword and scales in her hand. The jewels sparkling in her robe, like stars in the still of truedark. Those black, pitiless eyes.

"*O, Black Mother, what do I do now?*"

The crowd was thunder.

It reverberated through the stone around her, echoed on the sweat-slick walls. Dust drifted down from the wooden beams above, the rumble of thousands of feet, the tremor of their applause, the deafening peals of their adulation all around her, crawling on her skin and vibrating in the pit of her belly.

Mia had never heard anything like it in all her life.

She stood in the holding cell beneath the arena, peering out through the bars to the sands beyond. Matteo stood beside her, dark eyes wide in wonder. Sidonius paced up and down their little cell, like a caged beast longing to be unleashed. Or perhaps, longing to run. Mia looked at the word COWARD branded into his chest. Wondered what exactly he'd done to earn it.

"You ever attended a *venatus,* little Crow?" he asked.

"My father would never allow it. He thought the games were barbaric."

Sidonius looked out to the mob and nodded. "A wise man."

"Not *that* wise . . ."

The wagon ride from Crow's Nest to Blackbridge had taken almost a week. As ever, Mia, Matteo and Sidonius had been kept apart from the true gladiatii, and none of them deigned to speak a word to her. They'd been well fed, however, and perhaps out of some sympathy for what was to come, Butcher had refrained from pissing in any more dinners. After six turns, they'd arrived in the shadows of the Drakespine Mountains, and rolled into the sprawling metropolis of Blackbridge.*

---

*A city situated in the Drakespine Mountains, Blackbridge was the site of one of the most infamous sieges in Itreyan history.

Set on forging the greatest kingdom the world had seen, the Great Unifier, Francisco I, first set his sights on the Kingdom of Vaan. When word reached the Vaanian king, Brandr VI, that Francisco was marching his War Walkers toward his kingdom, he sent two of his most loyal captains—Halfstad and Ulfr—to hold the line at Blackbridge.

Nestled in a valley in the Drakespine, the city was shielded on all sides by great granite peaks, and accessible from the south by a single stone bridge for which the city was named. Halfstad, who was elderly at the time, gave command of the walls to his daughter, the shield-maiden Eydis. Ulfr, a much younger man, commanded the guerilla troops that harried Francisco's troops in the field. The siege was hard and tempers among the Vaanians were stretched, but still, they managed to fend off the Itreyan assault for six months. With wintersdeep setting in, Francisco's great general, Valerian, declared Blackbridge to be impregnable.

Sadly, the same could not be said of Halfstad's daughter, Eydis.

In the six months cooped up in the city, Eydis and Ulfr had grown rather fond of each other, you see. But when Eydis informed her father she was pregnant by his ally, old Halfstad took the news worse than anyone had expected. Declaring Ulfr had besmirched his daughter's honor, he attacked his fellow hüslaird in the city square. Ulfr's men leapt to their laird's defense, Halfstad's men joined the fray to protect their own,

Now, they waited under the city's great arena. The first exhibitions were under way—public murders sponsored by the local administratii. Mia watched as the sands were baptized with blood, convicted criminals and heretics and escaped slaves being executed *e gladiatii,* whetting the crowd's appetite for the bloodshed to come.

The Blackbridge arena was huge, elliptical, four hundred feet long. It seated at least twenty thousand people, the sunslight kept off the crowd by moving mekwerk canvases overhead. The stalls and bleachers were packed, folk traveling from miles around to witness the blood and glory of the *venatus.* Mia could see vendors selling salted meats and wine. Wives sitting with husbands, children riding on their parents' shoulders for a better view.

Nothing brings the familia together like a nice afternoon of slaughter.

As common chattel, Mia and the other recruits were scheduled to fight first. The Winnowing was always a bloody spectacle, and the editorii always tried to put on a good show for the mob. But the crowd still favored bouts between their heroes over the mass slaughter of nameless wretches, no matter how impressive their murders. The bouts featuring *true* gladiatii would be fought afterward, once the Winnowing was done.

Staring out at the blood-soaked sand, Mia felt herself trembling. The long-forgotten sensation of fear was swelling in her gut, turning her legs to water. The absence of Mister Kindly and Eclipse was a gnawing emptiness. An almost physical pain. She gripped the bars to still her shaking hands, cursing herself a coward.

You fought to be here. All this, your design. And now you stand there, trembling like a fucking child . . .

She pictured Duomo and Scaeva presiding over her father's execution in the forum. The baying crowd, howling for her father's blood. Looking out into the arena seats, she saw those same faces, that same awful delight. The same kind of people who cheered for her father's death.

But not for mine, you bastards. This is not where I die.

She curled her fingers into fists.

I've far too much killing to do.

---

and before anybody knew what was happening, the Vaanian forces were venting six month's frustration and murdering each other by the hundreds.

Both hüslairds perished in the fracas. Blackbridge fell to the Itreyans shortly afterward, which opened the entire country for invasion. Within two years, Vaan became the first vassal state of the great Kingdom of Itreya.

And if you can find me a better endorsement for the rhythm method, gentlefriends, I shall eat my pen.

"Recruits," came a voice.

Mia turned, saw Executus at the cell door. Instead of his usual leather armor and whip, he was dressed in britches and a fine doublet, set with the red falcon of the Familia Remus and the golden lion of the Familia Leonides. His long gray hair was braided, his beard combed—if not for the scar slicing down his face and the iron leg, he might have been mistaken for a wealthy don out for an afternoon's sport.

"Now is the hour," he said, his voice grave. "Death or glory awaits. It shall be for you to decide which is given, and which received."

Matteo spoke with a trembling voice. "What shape will the Winnowing take?"

"The editorii will announce once you are in position. But no matter the challenge, the way to victory is always the same." He gave a soft shrug. "Don't get killed."

Matteo looked ready to spew his mornmeal all over his sandals. Sidonius was pacing again, running his hand over his stubbled scalp. Mia shifted her weight, one foot to another, sick to her stomach.

The executus looked among them, and for the first time, Mia thought she saw the tiniest hint of softness in his eyes.

"Every gladiatii once stood where you stand now," he said. "Myself among them. No matter what you face on those sands, fear is the only enemy in your path. Conquer your fear, and you can conquer the world."

He placed his hand on his chest. Nodded once.

"*Sanguii e Gloria*. I will see you after the Winnowing as blooded gladiatii, or by the Hearth when I go to my eternal sleep. Aa watch over you, and Tsana guide your hand."

Arena guards in black armor marched into the cell, escorted Mia and the others down a long corridor. She heard trumpets signaling the end of the executions. A roar echoed above their heads in response. Through the walls and beneath her feet, Mia heard the creak and groan of metal on metal, the grinding of mighty gears.

"What *is* that?" Matteo whispered.

"Mekwerk beneath the arena floor," Mia replied. "The editorii control everything that happens on the sands from the underbelly."

"You know an awful lot about the *venatus* for a girl who's never attended one," Sidonius muttered.

Mia tried to smile mysteriously in reply, but couldn't quite manage it for the butterflies in her belly.

They were marched into a larger holding pen, sealed with a great iron portcullis. Beyond, Mia could see the blistering sunlight, and the waiting arena. The sands daubed in crimson. The crowd swaying and rolling like water.

The room was filled with perhaps forty others, lined up in orderly rows. Each was handed a heavy iron helm with a tall crest of scarlet horsehair, a short steel gladius and a broad rectangular shield daubed with a red crown. No armor. Nothing to protect the rest of her skin but the strips of fabric around her hips and chest. Mia looked among the mob, saw folk of every color and size, mostly men, a handful of women. In their eyes, she saw fervor, she saw fury, she saw fatalism.

But most of all, she saw fear.

"When the doors open," bellowed a guard in a centurion's plume, "take your place upon the sands and upon the stage of history! *Sanguii e Gloria!*"

"Four Daughters, I'm not ready for this . . . ," Matteo whispered.

"Stay staunch," Mia said, squeezing his hand. "Stay beside me."

"You have a plan, little Crow?" Sidonius murmured.

Trumpets sounded again, the crowd roaring in answer.

"Aye." She swallowed thickly. "Don't get killed."

A voice rang out across the arena, loud as the bellowing crowd.

"Citizens of Itreya! Honored administratii! Senators and marrowborn! Welcome to the forty-second *venatus* of Blackbridge!"

The roof above Mia's head shook, dust falling as the folk on the bleachers overhead thundered in reply.

"In honor of Governor Salvatore Valente, we present epic contest between heroic gladiatii of the finest collegia in the Republic! But first, those who seek glory upon the sands must be proved worthy before the eyes of the Everseeing! The time is nigh! The hour has come! The Winnowing is here!"

Mia pushed her helm down onto her head, checked her gladius, missing Mister Kindly like a hole in her chest.

Conquer your fear, and you can conquer the world . . .

"Behold!" came the cry. "As we present to you, the Siege of Blackbridge!"

Applause came then, almost deafening. But beneath the crowd's fervor, Mia heard the great grinding under the floor rising in pitch. A commotion broke out in the front ranks, men and women pushing forward against the portcullis to see. Before Mia's wondering eyes, the arena floor split apart, and a small keep made of stone began rising from the mechanism in the stadium's underbelly.

"Four Daughters," Matteo breathed. "Is that a . . . castle?"

Other parts of the floor split asunder, hidden platforms rising as the great